THE TWO SISTERS

The viscount rose from the table, pulling Julia to her feet and led her, in spite of her protests, towards a divan on which he deposited her on her knees with her head buried in the cushions.

'Stay there,' he ordered, 'I am the master.'

With an expert hand, he turned up her skirts as you would those of a little girl about to be spanked. The soft folds of her dress fell about her head like a cloche.

'Don't move,' he said, as the bottom of the slip joined the skirts and two charming buttocks emerged from the billows of cambric and lace.

Gaston then tore a long fringe of silk off the divan and set about punishing her. However the strokes were administered so gently and so accurately that they produced nothing more than a voluptuous tickling sensation . . .

Also available

THE TWO SISTERS

Anonymous

Translated from the French by
Frank Pomeranz

NEXUS

A Nexus Book
Published in 1988
by the Paperback Division of
W. H. Allen & Co. Plc
44 Hill Street, London W1X 8LB

Translation copyright © Nexus Books 1988
Printed in Great Britain by
Cox & Wyman Ltd, Reading, Berks.

ISBN 0 352 32017 6

Translator's dedication:
For Jasna Dilevska, my own lost Julia.
F.P.

Publisher's Note

The Two Sisters is a new translation of a well-known French erotic novel *Les Cousines de la Colonelle*. The book was first published in two volumes – Volume One appeared in Brussels in 1880 and Volume Two in Paris in 1882. Despite the frequent attribution of the novel to Guy de Maupassant, authorities credit the work to the literary hostess and friend of the poet Verlaine, the Marquise de Mannoury d'Ectot. It is thought that Mannoury d'Ectot is also responsible for another erotic work, *Violette*, which is also available in this series.

VOLUME ONE

CHAPTER ONE

One of those downpours of needle-sharp, icy rain that December often has up its sleeve was deluging the city. The rue d'Assas was practically deserted. Inside the houses, the splashing of water running through the gutters could be heard and the wind, howling lugubriously, buffeted the already cheerless suburb.

In Madame Briquart's small drawing-room, four people were gathered: the lady of the house, a respectable colonel's widow, who carried her sixty years as vigorously as – it was said – she had worn the trousers in the lifetime of her husband, who was brave only when he was at the head of his regiment. Not that Madame Briquart was, or looked like, a battleaxe; far from it, she was a frail creature with mild manners and winning ways but she was one of those women whose eye betrayed calm and unwavering determination. Blended with this, there was also that tolerance which experience of life develops in people of superior intelligence.

Seated close to her were Julia, her young niece, who was idly leafing through an album, and Florentine, Julia's sister, who was busy with her embroidery.

As they listened to a gentleman of about fifty, known as Cousin George, reading a novel by Octave Feuillet, the three women followed their own train of thought which, that evening, was slightly tinged with sadness.

A particularly strong gust of wind shook the house.

Madame Briquart curled up in her armchair and gave the luxurious shiver of someone whose sense of well-being was enhanced by the atrocious weather beyond her four walls. All those in the room had similar feelings, though they expressed them in different ways.

Julia looked up and said, 'What ghastly weather!'

Florentine lowered her head over her needlework like a lily bowing its fragrant head of petals to the wind.

George interrupted his reading, first to look at Florentine and then to say with a complacent laugh, 'It's a good deal pleasanter being in your drawing-room, Aunt, than in the middle of the Champs-Elysées, isn't it?'

'Yes, indeed,' the old lady said; 'and I am certain that our friends will let us have our tea all by ourselves tonight.'

'You'd have to be mad or in love – and that's more or less the same thing – to come to the rue d'Assas, at the far end of a remote suburb, on a night like this when the streets are awash like mill-streams.'

'People in love don't find their way here,' Julia said.

'Really?', George Vaudrez said somewhat challenging-ly. 'Are you quite sure about that?'

'Positive. You can go on reading your tale of this lady, whose readiness for self-sacrifice – it seems to me – borders on madness, without the slightest fear of interruption.'

As soon as she had spoken, the sound of a carriage drawn by two horses, whose rhythmical gait betrayed their breeding, made itself heard; it stopped abruptly outside the house and the doorbell rang.

'Surely it can't be anyone for us in this foul weather,' Madame Briquart said.

Before anyone could answer, the drawing-room door opened and the maid announced Viscount Saski, the mention of whose name slightly deepened the creases on George's forehead and suffused Julia's cheeks with a rosy hue – unless it was the fresh air coming through the open door that did that.

'How charming of you to brave this gale and come to see us,' Madame Briquart said, extending her wrinkled hand, over which – in accordance with a custom now old-fashioned in France but still considered charming in Russia and Poland – the young man bent his head in order to kiss it respectfully.

'A walk in Kamchatka would seem delightful to me if I knew we would meet,' the viscount replied gallantly. He addressed his hostess but his eyes, looking over her head, spoke even more eloquently to Julia.

'You are a flatterer, but who am I to scold you when you so bravely faced the storm and came to the end of town to take tea with recluses like us.'

The conversation continued in this vein for some time but then the young man gradually got closer to Julia and they started to chat quietly.

A sort of chill seemed to have descended on the company with the young man's arrival. George had fallen silent and Florentine abandoned her needlework to leaf through the book George had left on the table. Madame Briquart glanced at the company with a somewhat pointed look and then, remembering her manners, desisted, but nobody noticed. Julia took a keen interest in Saski's conversation, while Florentine was fully occupied by George who pointed out passages in 'The Diary of a Woman' which had been underlined in pencil.

Eleven o'clock struck. Coralie, the maid, brought in a tray of tea things and the girls did the honours. By midnight the doorkeeper was able to note that the last of his quiet tenants' guests had departed and that he himself could now safely abandon himself to the solace of sleep.

Several weeks passed, as alike as peas in a pod to the three ladies we have described, bringing no change in their existence. But, all the same, a crisis was brewing, which was to affect their lives drastically.

Julia and Florentine were the daughters of a first cousin of Madame Briquart's, who had from childhood on felt a sentiment for him that is difficult to describe, one of more than affection and less than love. Whatever it was, there was an extremely strong bond between them which nothing could break. Nothing at all? Well, yes, death could.

And it was death that snatched away poor Hector, a widower of two years' standing, without leaving him enough time to do more than send his two little girls to Madame Briquart with a note saying, 'I am dying. Please take them in.'

She took them in and brought them up, worrying from time to time about the future of these charming creatures whom she loved like a mother.

'Young, beautiful and penniless,' she would muse. 'I can see only perilous reefs and bad times ahead.'

That day she had picked at her chop and scarcely touched the half bottle of Chambertin she normally had with each meal for medical reasons.

When coffee had been cleared away, Madame Briquart looked at Florentine and asked her almost sharply, 'Have you any rooted objection to matrimony?'

6

The young woman looked up, blushed and replied with a smile, 'Not at all, Aunt, but of course it depends on who I'd share my life with.'

'I see. Well, it's with someone who worships you.'

'Someone who worships her? Have you a snippet of news then, Aunt?' Julia said with a laugh and then, turning to her sister, 'Get ready for something terrible.' Addressing her aunt once again, she asked, 'Is there a proposal in the wind? Don't keep us on tenterhooks, Aunt.'

'Far be it from me to do that. I'll tell you straight out without beating about the bush. Cousin George had a long talk with me yesterday, during which he expressed the warmest sentiments for Florentine and asked for her hand. The only answer I could give him was that I would faithfully pass on his message. Now it's up to you to decide. George is my late husband's nephew, and I have known him for twenty-five years. He is well off, reasonably personable, intelligent enough to manage his affairs competently and has always behaved like a perfect gentleman. As for you, you are young and good looking but, at present, far from rich and will be even less so in future. I invested all my husband left me in an annuity to keep all three of us in reasonable comfort but it will come to an end with my death. So the time has come to think seriously about the future. What do you feel about George?'

Florentine had paled a little. At twenty, a girl's dream suitor is scarcely likely to be a man of fifty-five. She was very fond of Monsieur Vaudrez, whom she had regarded as a relation ever since she had been a little girl, though in fact they were no kin at all. But her pulse had never once raced in his presence and, despite his flattering attentions, it had never once crossed her mind that one day she might become his lifelong companion. She was a sweet young thing and completely innocent in matters of love. True, in her reading, she had come across more glittering prospects than those held out to her now but she felt no anguish or repugnance at the thought of giving her tiny hand in matrimony to George Vaudrez.

'You know more about life than I, Aunt,' she said after a moment's hesitation. 'Please arrange things as you think best.'

'What that means is "I don't love George madly, but I like him enough to accept the agreeable position he offers me, in spite of his fifty-five years." '

'I don't know that that's quite right . . . It's rather that I would be happy to give the good Monsieur Vaudrez pleasure.'

'Well, that's rich,' Julia exclaimed, 'marrying a man just to give him pleasure! Who's ever heard of such a thing? There are love matches, marriages of convenience and even marriages to atone for some wrong – but marriages merely for the sake of being obliging are absolutely unheard of! You have my best wishes, little sister, but I shall never follow your example.'

'You may live to regret that one day,' her aunt said. 'Luckily we are not talking about you but about Florentine and I shall lose no time in making George blissfully happy by telling him that she will allow him to pay his addresses to her.'

Madame Briquart got up and left the dining-room; the girls followed her example and each went to her own bed-room to ponder on the events of the morning.

A marriage creates quite a stir in a household. The prospect of hers worried Florentine rather less than it did her sister. Not that Julia envied her; she loved her too much for that. She was too good-natured, high-minded and sincerely devoted to Florentine to harbour such sentiments. However, Madame

Briquart's remarks, which had allowed them a glimpse into their true position – and until then Julia had not even given it a thought – produced a welter of worrying reflections.

'Being without a fortune,' she said to herself, 'is tantamount to being condemned to live out one's life as an old maid or to be the wife of an infatuated dotard or an idiot. Who else would marry a girl without a dowry in this fair land of France? What a prospect! All the same, I am not resigned to it. Everything in nature keeps repeating the word *love;* am I to forswear its glow for ever? And all this for a quiet life, a tame existence full of little everyday cares and regular, expected, and insipid satisfactions. Never! Never! Never!'

This declaration, resounding like a clarion call in her mind, was met by a sombre, low voice, which asked,

'And what if you don't find a young, handsome, rich, loving husband?'

That discordant note remained unanswered.

Florentine, for her part, experienced no such worries. She quickly collected herself and in her mind's eye saw the life of a *châtelaine*, a prospect she found entirely pleasing. George lived for most of the year in a country house near Paris, which she knew well, as she had spent a good many holidays there. She could see herself enthroned in the grand drawing-room, doing the honours when entertaining guests. The mornings were all gilded with sunshine and scented with country fragrances which she breathed in greedily as she attended to the everyday tasks of country life and the important matter of giving orders to the servants.

At noon, she would be surrounded by her family, presiding over the luncheon table in the midst of toddlers gambolling round her and calling her 'Mama'. This idyllic scene was completed by a white-haired George benevolently observing it and looking at her with eyes of love. This vision of the future had so completely captured her mind and her heart that she gladly put her hand in George's that evening and gave him the answer he had so devoutly desired – *yes*.

Madame Briquart did not want to seem to rush things, but she thought it best that the engagement should not be drawn out too long and her nephew raised no objection to this. For the next six weeks, there were constant comings and goings by dress-makers and seamstresses. Madame Briquart was very open-handed in the way she did things.

'All I'm giving you is your trousseau, so let it at least be pretty.'

And it was with meticulous care that the good lady chose all the fetching négligés, fine beribboned cambrics and the thousand trifles which go to make the accompaniment of nights of love.

'But, Aunt,' Florentine would object from time to time, 'why take so much trouble over things nobody will ever see?'

The old lady smiled and merely said, 'Just let me have my little pleasures.'

Madame Briquart knew the ways of the world and she was not ignorant of the fact that her nephew was a great sinner before the Lord, having in the past made generous use of the privileges he enjoyed as a bachelor. When young, and even after that, he had spent his leisure hours in company that was more voluptuous than intellectual and which preferred extreme indulgence to finer spiritual feelings – usually absent or at least rare among the priestesses of Venus. She did not want the new husband to be exposed to the same temptations as the old bachelor; she remembered a couple whose future path had at the outset seemed to be strewn with roses but who had, a mere fortnight later, been at each other's throats, merely because the young wife, ill-advised by her mother, had on the wedding night displayed a pair of unbleached lisle stockings with a night-dress to match. So she spared no pains or money.

Finally the great day dawned. Delightful to look at in her orange-blossom crown, enveloped in billows of white lace, Florentine faithfully promised love and fidelity to her husband. She felt a little emotional, but not at all fearful, when after luncheon among friends, she mounted the carriage that was to take them to their country house where George had, in agreement with Madame Briquart, decided to spend the first few hours of their wedded bliss.

George was not one of those people who subscribed to the newfangled fashion of enjoying the most impressionable moments of life in all sorts of outlandish places, or of letting the four walls of some impersonal hotel witness the first blossoming of a young bride. No, he preferred that memories of their own home, where their life was to be spent and where – if it were to please God to grant them that boon – their children would be born, should in moments of distress (and everyone is subject to them now and then) give strength and succour to whichever of them was at that time in need of such comfort.

CHAPTER TWO

The brougham made good time and soon the ramparts of Paris were lost in the mists behind them. George had taken one of his wife's hands into his two and pressed it tight; from time to time he bestowed a kiss on her brow, which was received without blushes or embarrassment. All this was very chaste, much more so, if the truth were told, than the bridegroom would have wished.

Monsieur Vaudrez was not the sentimental type. Essentially he was a sensualist and, in marrying Florentine, he had hoped first and foremost to revive sensations which he had found more and more difficult to experience as time went on. At the same time, like a one-time gourmet, he wanted to sample once more the delicacies he had been missing for some while and which were now going to be at his disposal.

For two fine horses, it was not a long way from Paris to Montmorency, near which *Les Charmettes*, the Vaudrez country house, was situated, and they were soon there.

The new husband had seen to it that there would hardly be anyone about when they arrived. The only person the young bride met was a discreet and obliging lady's maid with an expression of intelligence and impeccable gravity but with eyes which spoke volumes.

The bed-room suite set aside for Florentine had been refurbished and contained a collection of the most charming bibelots.

'How kind you are,' the young woman said with conviction when, after a most civilised dinner, she was back in her rooms and offering a cup of tea to her husband of a few hours' standing.

'Not at all. It is you who are kind, my best beloved, who have entrusted your life to my care. Yes, you are the kind one. How I long to take possession of my darling wife!'

'I don't understand. Aren't you my lord and master already?'

'Not completely, my love. All I've done is to acquire the right to become . . . as you put it, your lord and master.'

Is the dear child really completely innocent? – George said to himself – could Madame Briquart really have missed this excellent opportunity of letting her imagination dwell on what had long ago become forbidden fruit to her? Surely not! Still, it'll be best to be circumspect.

'Do you think, my pet, that what happened at the registry office and the church this morning make up the supreme joys of love?'

The young woman blushed and lowered her head.

'I don't know,' she murmured.

How sweet she is, George thought; what a delight it will be to pluck that flower of innocence.

'Really?' He said aloud. 'Well, I'll instruct you. But wouldn't you like to get more comfortable? Those stays must constrict you. Do you need your maid's help to take them off?'

'Oh, no.'

'In that case, let's tell her she's not wanted any

13

more tonight and attend to our little affairs all by ourselves.'

So Mariette was dismissed for the night and George bolted the doors of the suite.

Florentine had already gone into the dressing-room to follow the advice she had been given. George, hidden behind a screen, was watching her and his blood became heated at the sight of her arms and shoulders which, uncovered, showed all their youthful splendour. When she had nothing left on but her shift, he suddenly emerged from his hiding-place and took her in his arms.

'Gracious, how you startled me,' the young woman exclaimed, disconcerted and blushing.

Deep down she had known that a woman's life concealed some mystery but she had no idea what this unknown thing was that both her aunt and her father confessor had told her had now become her duty, towards the successful performance of which, the two of them had preached complete submission to the wishes of her husband.

George was very pale. He took her in his arms and smothered her lips, shoulders and breasts – which she tried in vain to hide from his view – with kisses. Suddenly, his fingers slid along the length of her body and seized the delicious protuberances below the small of her back; he writhed with voluptuous desire as he put his dry and ardent mouth against her rose-coloured lips.

Then, roaming further still, he managed, in spite of the young woman's efforts to regain possession of her body, to hug her thighs and knees. Two white velvet garters held up the fine silk mesh covering her legs; he undid them and let the underclothes still covering the lower part of her delicate figure slide to the floor. Florentine, like a scared bird, emitted little cries of alarm and fled to the far end of the room.

'Florentine, my darling, are you frightened of me to run away from me like that? Am I not your husband? Why won't you be my wife?'

'I don't understand. Is there more to come still?'

'Come here then, my love; I'll explain to you what the difference between a man and a woman consists of.'

'I daren't, like this,' the young wife said, looking unhappily at her very scanty costume.

'What are you worried about, my child? Not the way you are dressed, surely? – it is the most beautiful in the world, specifically reserved for feasts of love. I'll tell you what I'll do to make you feel better. I, too, will remove everything that might stand in the way of the ardour of our amatory transports.'

Suiting the action to his words, George immediately divested himself of all his outer clothing and stood beside his wife in a similar state of undress.

'Come,' he said, hugging her with a caressing arm and drawing her on to a sofa, 'there, close to me . . . that's it. I shall tell you what my love requires of yours – because you do love me, my beautiful, adorable little wife, and you will go on loving me. You must often have read in the Bible that a man and his wife are one flesh and blood when they are united in wedlock.'

'Yes, I have.'

'Well then, how does this come about? Not by letting your husband take possession of the treasures concealed in your bosom, beyond this charming hemisphere which I am caressing at this moment, but of those down here, in the very depths of your being, at the entrance of which my hand is now – at the spot where I am putting my finger.'

George had seized the young novice with his left

arm and held her half recumbent, while his right hand was busy exploring and giving tactile demonstrations, which Florentine began to react to with pleasurable excitement.

'So that you should be wholly mine, my treasure, I must penetrate you.'

'But how is that to be done?'

'So you don't know how a man's body differs from a woman's?'

'No.'

'Well then, hold this in your hand, finger it and look at it.'

George took out his perforator, the instrument God had placed at the disposal of his male creatures to enable them to exercise their dominion, and the frightened young woman had to pass her little hand over her husband's rigid phallus.

'You are the quiver for this fine arrow, which will triumphantly enter you to make your womb fruitful and initiate you into all the delightful mysteries of love.

Now that you know this, will you be my wife? Will you make good the promise you gave me this morning?'

'Yes,' she murmured in a scarcely audible voice.

'You will need to be brave because – do you see? – the first skirmish of love is a struggle; the door to paradise is locked and I must break it down.'

George did not wait for an answer; he seized Florentine in his arms, drew her into the bedroom and laid her on the huge bed, which was waiting to become the scene of their frolics.

Then, with a vigorous leap, he lay down beside her, stretching his hirsute legs out alongside her body, made moist, supple and intoxicated by contact with him; finally, he got on top of her, spread her thighs, which – out of innocence or fear – had been locked together, and said to himself – the hour of victory is at hand.

Monsieur Vaudrez was still very vigorous and could play a brilliant part in guerilla warfare, but set battles, like this one, were a different matter and required a soldier to be in perfect condition, as he discovered to his horror. The struggle and the explanations had taken a certain amount of time and the proud state of the bridegroom had undergone a worrying change. Debility had taken over from vigour and it was now going to be impossible to capture the fortress, ready to surrender though it was.

What a fool I've been, he told himself, not to have accepted the invigorating drops Albert offered me. That good friend told me I was wrong to refuse. And, good Lord, how right he was! Luckily my wife is as innocent as a new-born babe, so I'll be able to fob her off with second best.

So he continued to busy himself outside the sanctuary and suddenly felt the charming little button of love his perfidious friend was tickling stiffen and swell; stifled moans came from Florentine's lips, as she writhed like a serpent. George was no novice: he understood the situation – charming and shameful at the same time. He took the delinquent member in one hand and by judicious rubbing soon produced his own paroxysm of love. The young woman cried out. George had come on the threshold of the holy of holies. She was still a virgin but had ceased to be entirely innocent, for she had just experienced the first sensations of love.

George was furious. He had failed. He looked sadly at his wife, half unconscious on the bed, and the pitiful state she was in. He lay down close to her, hoping that Cupid would yet come to his aid, and . . . fell fast asleep.

As for Florentine, who was tired by these first nervous exertions, she too had a good rest and next morning it was with a radiant face that, on waking, she was bold enough to plant a kiss on her husband's lips. Marriage did not seem such a terrible thing to her and she had only the most pleasant recollections of her wedding night. George did not feel sufficiently restored from his exertions of the previous night to attempt a new battle. So he decided once more to use a ruse and to respond to the caresses of Florentine, who was fondly pressing against him, by re-enacting the scene of the night before. His finger strayed to the young woman's golden, marmalade-cat-like fleece, stopped at the key of erotic sensation, vibrated it in its velvet lock and then, not without causing a little pain, it went on in the direction of the sanctuary itself, where it took note of the difficulties of the final battle during which its owner would, if he did not want to be a laughing stock, have to do or die. This time, Florentine, a little more experienced now, readily lent herself to her husband's efforts and was rewarded with a climax more prolonged and delicious still than the first.

Tomorrow I shall get my drops and that'll be the end of it, George thought. That swine, Albert, will make fun of me, for sure, but never mind; the important thing is not to weaken half-way.

Albert was away from Paris and would not be back until the following day. So it was decided that Jean, the coachman, would call on Albert with a message on the way to collect Madame Briquart and Julia, who had accepted an invitation to come and dine at *Les Charmettes*.

18

CHAPTER THREE

At about two o'clock, George's carriage returned with
Madame Briquart and Julia. Time had hung heavily
on their hands: they had been consumed with curiosity. Madame Briquart remembered – Julia specu-
lated. Both were anxious to know how Florentine had
come through the crisis, of the probable vicissitudes
of which the aunt was well aware and which Julia
imagined to have been horrific, without being
tempered by any degree of pleasure, this being ruled
out by George's age.

Truth to tell, they were slightly disappointed by the
composure with which the young woman welcomed
them. She was pink and smiling, with just a hint of
crimson on her cheeks when she sensed her aunt's
quizzical eye observing her. As for George, he looked
no different from usual, the blue rings round his eyes,
etched in by past dissipation, being no deeper than
was normal. Madame Briquart took in these details
which gave her food for deep thought. Well, well, she
said to herself, could he be fitter than I had supposed?

Cousin George fussed round the ladies and seemed
anxious not to leave his wife alone with her sister but
as someone once said, 'Whatever a woman wants,
God and the devil want it, too.' Here there were three
of them, so what could poor George do? He was forced
to do what he tried to avoid, on pain of seeming

ridiculous; he had to go and give orders to the servants, which Florentine, because she did not yet know the domestic staff, could not be expected to do.

Madame Briquart took advantage of this by drawing her niece into the latter's bed-room and, while Julia examined the thousand and one details of her sister's trousseau in the large glass-fronted wardrobes in the dressing room, made Florentine sit beside her on a *chaise longue*.

'Well, my poor little darling,' she said, affectionately squeezing both her niece's hands, 'how do you find marriage?'

'Very good, Aunt; George is most obliging and tender to me.'

'I can well believe it. But what about yourself?'

'Me? I feel very happy and see no reason why my happiness should not go on indefinitely.'

'Nor do I, my dear. But, tell me, was he brutal to you? A man — even the best of them — is at certain times — less than delicate. Do you understand?'

'George, brutal? Certainly not. He is full of attentions and solicitude.'

'Good, I can see that everything went well and that you haven't suffered too much. George must have consulted his doctor (Madame Briquart was going to relate her own experiences but thought better of it, so she brought the doctor into the conversation) and got him to give him a lubricant and a pain-killing lotion.'

'Whatever for, Aunt?'

'My dear child, to save you pain, of course, which always accompanies the first skirmish of love in women. The creator has decreed that struggle shall be the price of every triumph, and blood has to be shed for the sake of the first sensations of love as well as for the joys of motherhood.'

Madame Briquart was fond of being discursive; she

might well have continued in this vein, had her niece not interrupted her by saying,

'My dear Aunt, I don't understand a word of what you are saying. As we are speaking woman to woman (the young wife pronounced the words 'woman to woman' with such an air of gravity that it made the old lady smile), I can tell you that I had a delightful physical sensation; that this occurred without any struggle and without bloodshed; what is more, it happened twice in exactly the same way.'

'Go on with you . . .'

A ghastly thought struck Madame Briquart but she dismissed it as fantastic as soon as it was formed. No, this girl had never left her side since her childhood and the artlessness with which she described her impressions were proof of her integrity and chastity. Intuitively, she grasped the situation and said to herself: the devil, perhaps my nephew is less vigorous than I had thought.

'In that case, my pet, your husband has not yet availed himself of his conjugal rights. He probably did not want to scare you. That must be it.'

'But he did, Aunt. He really did.'

'In that case I don't understand what is going on.'

'Why not? It's wrong to feign ignorance. After all, you were married yourself and my uncle must have availed himself of his conjugal rights.'

'Indeed he did – so much so that four days after our wedding night a doctor had to be called in, because he had been so rough in turning a girl into a woman.'

'Does that mean that I'm not a woman yet, Aunt?'

'I don't think so, darling. You are still just a foolish virgin, at least I believe so.'

'I want to know for sure . . . ,' Florence mumbled.

The aunt drew the young woman to herself, half lay her down on her knees and, sliding her finger under Florentine's skirts, she lightly touched her clitoris, which raised its little pink head. She then passed on with caressing movements between the lips of the vulva and tried to penetrate into the vagina but was met by an impassable barrier.

'You are hurting me, Aunt.'

'Now you can see that you have to suffer to become a woman because you won't be one until George, by strong and repeated thrusts of his male member, which I presume he has, has pierced this membrane, which is called the hymen. Then you will have the delightful sensation, which you haven't experienced yet, of his plunging into your very depths and flooding you with the hot elixir of love that he carries within him and that will make fruitful your virginal womb. But blood has to flow and you have to pay for the delights of love and of motherhood with a few transitory moments of pain. George must have wanted to spare you.'

'All the same, Aunt, I did feel . . .'

'Just what you are going to feel now.'

And the old lady, by moving her skilful finger around the young woman's private parts, once again brought about that delightful climax which Florentine had supposed to be that of sexual possession.

'My God! Ah, it's as good as with George,' she murmured. 'Can a woman then . . . can she . . . well, can she make another woman happy?'

The aunt repressed the enigmatic smile that formed on her lips and discreetly pointed to the dressing-room door, through which Julia could no longer be heard rummaging in the wardrobes.

Florentine hastily adjusted her dress, gave her aunt a long kiss and called her sister, who at once appeared at the door with very red cheeks and an animated look.

'Well, my darling sister, did you like my bits and pieces? Didn't they make you want to get married too?'

'That depends on who to, but I confess I very much want to be loved, and to love also.'

'That'll come in time,' Madame Briquart said. 'I know a certain viscount who I suspect thinks like you.'

This time Julia became even more scarlet in the face. At that moment, there was a knock at the door and George's voice was heard asking whether he might come in.

'No, no,' he was told, 'we'll join you downstairs in a moment.'

George was on top of the world. Albert had come back to Paris and Jean, the coachman, had brought him the precious drops. He had taken them in accordance with the directions and was now digesting them together with the witty, but very bantering, letter that Albert had deemed it necessary to send along with them.

Dinner was consumed in a very jolly atmosphere. Madame Briquart could not resist dropping a hint or two questioning George's virility, which the latter pretended not to understand. 'The old witch', he said to himself; his feelings for his aunt were more affectionate than respectful. 'What' – he wondered – 'could she have said to my wife. Ah, my wife! We'll see tonight. I don't know whether it's the effect of the old Chambertin or whether it's the drops working but I can feel a stirring in my loins, even when merely looking at the venerable, and venerated, features of Madame Briquart.'

The ladies were doing justice to the champagne, of which George resolutely refused to touch a drop. The aunt thought: let's not say anything to him; he is evidently preparing for battle.

It had been decided that the ladies would spend a few days at *Les Charmettes*. Quite early, Madame Briquart announced she was tired and retired to her bedroom, asking Julia to join her in order to read to her, much to George's pleasure.

'My little darling,' he said to his wife, 'shall we follow your aunt's example? I feel a bit tired, too.'

'With pleasure.'

'Good. You go ahead and I'll join you when you have sent your maid away.'

George went to his own rooms, got into a tub and emptied a jug of iced water over his back, then over his whole body, paying special attention to his member which was destined for combat. He then carefully dried himself, rubbed his back, hips, arms, crutch and thighs with a sponge soaked in eau-de-Cologne, the vapour of which, in combination with the cold water, had a tonic effect. Having done this, he put on his dressing-gown, swallowed a cup of vanilla-scented tea, the aroma of which mingled with that of the drops that had been brought him, and, full of daring, flew to his wife's bed-room, which was separated from his only by their dressing-rooms.

Florentine was sitting up in her huge bed with its upholstered headboard, looking delightfully pretty in the midst of billows of lace and scented cambric: she was waiting for him with her elbows propped on the pillow, a little anxious about her second wedding night, which she felt instinctively would see her complete initiation into the mysteries of love.

This time, George did not make the mistake of indulging in the delights of a long prelude; in passing through his wife's dressing-room, he had seized a jar of cold cream and liberally applied it to himself. As soon as the heat of their intertwined bodies told him that a sort of magnetic communication had been established between them, he bestowed a few perfunctory caresses on his better half and then mounted his attack, determined not to be put off by any distraction. With an agile finger, he prepared her for the assault and, very proud of the state of tumescence in which he found himself thanks to the little cure he had undergone, he bounded forward, drawing a cry of pain from Florentine in the first shock.

'You must be brave, my darling; it is only at the cost of a few minutes' pain that I can make you happy. Help me and you'll suffer less. Push a little yourself.'

But for the conversation the young woman had had with Madame Briquart, she would no doubt have put up more resistance, but she was annoyed at the thought of still being a virgin; it had seemed to her that her aunt was making fun of her. She now felt more comfortable with her husband than the night before and she supported his efforts with a to-and-fro movement, interspersed with little moans which George muffled with his kisses; soon their movements, aided no doubt by the cold cream, became easier: dilatation took place and an energetic thrust brought about the sundering of the obstinate membrane. George's cry of triumph mingled with the wails of Florentine; she felt transfixed, but at the same time experienced a sensation of supreme pleasure. The pain ceased as the result of the internal caresses her husband lavished upon her; she seemed to feel something like a kiss inside her; then, something hot and delicious flooded her; the spasm with which she was already familiar came back to her but this time with quite unfamiliar intensity; her whole being trembled; she became unconscious of all that was going on round her and did not revive till a few moments later under the influence of George's kisses.

CHAPTER FOUR

Julia had not missed one word of the conversation between Madame Briquart and Florentine; at first, she had not been able to account for the silences, interrupted by sighs, that she had noticed but, by rapidly manipulating the cheval glass, she had got a glimmering of what until then had been quite outside her ken.

Indeed, her aunt's hand between Florentine's thighs had left no doubts in her mind. It occurred to her to ask her aunt that evening to clear up some of the details which she still did not fully understand. But then a biblical injunction crossed her mind: Seek and ye shall find. She promised herself to do just that in George's library next day. But as the dinner-gong had not yet sounded, she decided to examine visually the conformation of the female holy of holies, where the destinies of the world are determined.

She let the clouds of cambric enveloping her slide down to her pink and white feet and stood in front of the wardrobe mirror. At first, her nakedness made her nervous but then, when this feeling, inseparable from every new experience, had been dissipated, she gazed at the reflection of a beautiful statue in silent admiration. The young girl had visited too many museums and had too highly developed an aesthetic sense not to realise that she was face to face with the contours of a remarkably fine-looking woman.

Tall, slim and curvaceous, her supple figure, as if by instinct, adopted a voluptuous pose; the tips of her virgin breasts stood up in a startled way, their scarlet strawberries spotting the surrounding snow.

Julia was typical of those nervous, hot-blooded and fair-skinned brunettes, whose ardour is concealed within and rarely colours their skin. Her grotto of love, veiled by a curly jet-black fleece, quickly caught her attention. She had seen it clearly: it was there that her aunt had put her finger. This then must be the key to the mysteries of love, of which everything round her reminded her but of which she knew nothing, though she was older than Florentine. She caressed herself, slid her finger up and down but – inexperienced as she was – felt only a vague sort of excitation and enervation. She thought: there must be more to it than this; I want to find out what it is and I will. With this resolution uppermost in her mind, our seeker after knowledge fell asleep.

Long before the newly-weds and Madame Briquart had come down to breakfast, Julia was busy rummaging through the library. First of all, she found a delightful bucolic novel by Longus, which he had euphoniously called *Daphnis and Chloe*. Leafing through it at random, she came across the chapter describing the charming scene where the two *ingénus* try, by getting close to each other, to calm their ardent sensations but manage merely to arouse them still further. She shut the book and put it in her pocket to read at leisure later; then she went on with her researches.

She came across the extravagant pages – sizzling, wild and inflammatory – from the pen of Alfred de Musset and George Sand in their story, *Gamiani* she quickly read it through and saw what was to be seen in this volume, which it is a pity a more skilful hand was not found to illustrate. Her collection now seemed adequate to her and she took refuge in her bedroom.

Gamiani had been devoured well before luncheon. It seemed monstrous to her in some of its details: *Daphnis and Chloe* accorded better with her mood of the moment; she immersed herself in it and told herself: No, that still isn't it, I feel; the mystery of love does not speak to everyone in the same accents, but in the end I shall learn the language and speak it, too.

Through the reveries that followed this reflection, there suddenly loomed up the attractive vision of a charming man – obliging, gallant, dark-eyed – flashing looks at her capable of melting ice and starting conflagrations.

'Aunt, when are we going back to Paris?' Julia asked after luncheon.

'Whenever you like,' Madame Briquart said with some surprise. 'Are you in a hurry to leave? I thought you liked it at *Les Charmettes*.'

'Not at present. George and Florentine, I am sure, would prefer to be undisturbed, even by our presence.'

Madame Briquart did not entirely agree. If this had been a young couple, Julia's remark would have made good sense; but at George's age, congenial company was likely to make a pleasant change from an uninterrupted *tête-à-tête* with his young wife.

Julia was not one of those vacillating characters that bend to every breeze; on the contrary, she was extremely strong-willed, so, that evening, George's carriage took the two ladies back to the rue d'Assas.

The secret reason for the young woman's hurry to get back to Paris was that Madame Briquart's regular 'At Home' was due next day and she felt sure that

Viscount Saski would come to pay court to her. Nor did she turn out to be mistaken in this. He had himself announced at about half past nine, to show that he was devoting the evening entirely to her in preference to the opera, or any other entertainment that might have been in competition with her.

Julia had met the viscount several times; she was not unaware that he was in love with her but, that evening, he appeared to her in an entirely new light and a deep blush spread over her cheeks as she offered him her small hand, which he gallantly kissed. Her tenseness did not escape the attentive eyes of the viscount, who was no novice in matters of the heart and felt his pulse going faster in the presence of this young woman to whom he felt genuinely and deeply attracted.

There were enough people at Madame Briquart's that evening for a private conversation to be possible. Julia and the viscount took advantage of this but neither of them, usually so debonair, felt at ease: a kind of oppression weighed heavily upon them.

'What is the matter with you?' the young woman asked, in an attempt to distract herself from her malaise.

'I wanted to put the same question to you,' the young man said with a smile, 'but as you got in first, I shall tell you very, very softly what I should wish to have the right to shout out aloud. The matter with me, beloved Julia, is that I am madly in love with you. To think that we are here, obliged to talk in the presence of a score of others, and that the words of love my heart dictates to my lips have to be masked by a polite smile before they can reach your ears! All this, because absurd conventions prevent us from meeting without a chaperone and do not allow me to plead my cause, or to try to convince you that my life belongs to you, and that the possession of yours would make my happiness complete.'

The viscount did not tell the young woman anything she did not know already but this was the first time that he had clearly said: I love you. She experienced a delightful sensation of liberation, because she confessed to herself that she too loved the handsome and elegant young man, who spoke to her in terms as passionate as the present circumstances allowed and troubled her to the very depths of her soul.

'Now, that I have told you the reasons for my sense of oppression, Julia, won't you tell me yours, because you, too, seem ill at ease.'

'No, not here. We are talking of matters too serious for me to answer you here and now; like you, I feel that the language of the heart is profaned if spoken in the presence of indifferent people.'

Julia hesitated for a moment.

'The day after tomorrow,' she went on, 'my aunt is due to spend the afternoon and evening at *Les Charmettes;* I shan't go. Come along then and boldly tell Coralie that you have just met Madame Briquart who has given you a message to pass on to me.'

'You are an angel.'

'Me? Not at all. I am a woman, that's all. Is that not enough for you?'

'It's more than I deserve.'

'Come along, you conspirators, what are you plotting there without wigs or black masks?' asked Madame Briquart, who thought that the private conversation had gone on long enough. 'Help me do the honours at the tea-table.'

At midnight, when the guests had gone, Madame Briquart kissed her niece good-night and asked with a smile:

31

'What interesting things did our handsome Pole have to tell you? Did he by any chance think that orange blossom would suit your black tresses as well as it did Florentine's fair hair?'

'No doubt, he will tell you. Aren't you *in loco parentis* in matters of this kind?'

'It is, dear child, because I feel the affection and the sense of responsibility of a mother for you that I'd be happy to see you with an assured future. The viscount belongs to a very distinguished family and is rich enough to give you a secure future. If you like him, if you love each other, I should gladly give you my blessing. You must sail your ship as you think best. I am sure that whatever you do will be well done.'

'Thank you, Aunt,' Julia said, visibly moved but also relieved by the approval of the woman who had taken her dead parents' place in her life.

Next day she did not go out. The books she had read at *Les Charmettes* had borne fruit: the world of confused ideas that they had conjured up now fell into place and a ray of light, as it were, illuminated her mind. At the same time she had an overpowering desire to act out in real life the voluptuous acts described in the pages she had read.

This was the state of mind in which the viscount found her next day. Julia had had no difficulty in getting permission to stay behind when Madame Briquart drove to the country. She understood that her young niece was going through a profound crisis in a woman's life and needed to recover in solitude.

When the viscount called, as arranged, she received him in Madame Briquart's small private drawing-room, which the latter had designed in a very original and tasteful way and in Arab style. Fabric-covered walls and African carpets deadened the sound of voices and footsteps; large oriental divans were ranged along the walls and in the centre there was a pouffe-cum-sofa, with a *jardinière* above it, which made it possible to find a corner of the room sheltered from indiscreet eyes. This sanctum, established before the aunt's hair had turned white said a great deal more about her than the good colonel, who was not very bright, ever knew.

'Julia,' he said in an emotional tone of voice as soon as she had instructed Coralie to admit him, 'how good you are.'

'What do you know about that?', she said with a laugh. 'Perhaps you'll find me extremely wicked.'

There was a little embarrassment between them. This situation, entirely novel to Julia, of a *tête-à-tête* with a young man, made a tremendous impression on her.

As for him, he wanted the conversation to start as he meant to continue and, above all, he wanted to avoid all evasions and subterfuges. He was too much of a man of the world not to know that hesitation quickly becomes fatal to love in such circumstances. So he seized both the young woman's hands in his and looked her straight in the face, fascinating her with his smile and regard.

'Julia, my best beloved,' he said to her very gravely after a short silence, 'I told you yesterday that I love you. Look at me and tell me – do you love me, too? Tell me, my darling, my love, my life. Tell me, Julia, tell me,' he repeated in a feverish voice.

'Yes,' she stammered almost inaudibly.

She hid her head in Gaston's chest and he, maddened and drunk with happiness, smothered the trembling young woman's brow, hair, ears and neck with kisses. Suddenly, he seized her head in his two hands and planted on her two fiery lips one of those long kisses in which each drinks in the other's breath, which fuse two souls and create that supreme exhilaration that a sacred caress produces in young and ardent spirits — sacred because God permits it . . . and not to everybody.

Gaston was twenty-six. Like all northerners he did not wear his heart on his sleeve but, beneath his apparent reserve, there was a fiery temperament merely waiting to be released as soon as he felt his ardour was requited, which it certainly appeared to be to a greater extent than he had ever dared to hope. This went to his head, so that he felt he was seized by the sort of passion that goes to make criminals.

The young woman's bosom, which her light bodice protected inadequately, bounded on his chest; he felt that young flesh, instinctively greedy for love and voluptuousness, tremble and shiver; he lost his head and plunged his feverish hands into her half-unravelled hair, breathed in the scent emanating from it and stroked her hot arms with a hand which found no resistance.

He stood up, still caressing her, and sat on the divan, on to which Julia, oblivious of everything but the feeling of love which shook her from top to toe, soon fell in a half-swoon. Gaston let out a stifled cry, stood up again and pounced on her agitated bosom, the covering of which had slightly ridden up. He tore a button off the bodice, glued his lips to the delightful hemispheres now revealed to him without any of the mock modesty of those who do not know how to love well enough to do it proudly, conscious of the respect due to everything magnificent and beautiful.

Two stifled sighs, sounding like cries, escaped Julia, whose silence, apart from that, was more eloquent than the most passionate speeches. Gaston felt that his male member was at full stretch; adroitly he stripped it of its covering; then, after spreading the thighs of the young woman lying on the divan, he planted on the rose surrounded by fur, which met his gaze, a kiss which engulfed it practically in its entirety. He felt the love button of the woman who was giving herself to him swell under the influence of this kiss; changing course, he then tried to penetrate this fiery nest, which was going wild under his caresses, as deeply as possible, telling himself that the readiness with which she allowed things to be done to her would make it easy to cut the Gordian knot.

This, however, was a miscalculation.

But Julia, remembering the lesson her aunt had given her sister, lent herself to the viscount's movements in spite of the pain she was in. Suddenly a cry, immediately suppressed, escaped her to mingle with stifled sighs.

'Ah! I am suffering with happiness! Ah, my beloved, ah! This is heaven . . . I am dead . . . I . . .'

And this time, having well and truly fainted from the force of her spasm of love and the nervous shock she had sustained, she stayed motionless on the divan.

CHAPTER FIVE

The young woman came to quite quickly. Her first act was to put her arms round the viscount's neck and to bury her head in his chest.

'What have we done?' she murmured.

Gaston had recovered, too. He was extremely vexed with himself because he realised that he had rushed his courtship at an excessive pace. In wooing Julia, he had certainly not intended a seduction, pure and simple. He wanted to make her his companion for life, though he had no intention of marrying her yet for a number of reasons. The principal one was that, somewhere in the world, he had an old aunt, who had made it an absolute condition of his inheriting her wealth that he should await her death before tying, as she put it, the knot of matrimony.

So the precipitateness with which he had just acted and his moment of madness threatened to cost him 80,000 francs of income and reduce his budget to a minimum, that is to say about 30,000 francs, which in view of the company he kept and his life-style, amounted to straitened circumstances, bordering on indigence. For Gaston was a man of honour and had determined unhesitatingly to call on Madame Briquart next day and ask for her young niece's hand in marriage.

'Do you already regret having given yourself to me, my darling?' he asked.

'Not if you love me as much after as before.'

'A hundred times more, my beloved child.' He kissed her forehead. 'But, dear Julia, our union was such a sudden one that it has quite stunned me and I cannot help thinking about the various consequences that may spring from it, consequences it is my duty to consider.'

'Whatever you decide will seem good to me. I am yours, your object, your very soul. I shall approve of whatever you do.'

'My beloved, your confidence shall not be betrayed. Only, before seeing Madame Briquart to ask for your hand, I shall have to go away for a while because extremely grave matters oblige me to visit a relation, on whom I am partly dependent. But never fear, Julia, you are my wife and my arm will not fail you.'

'I don't understand,' Julia murmured, slightly ruffled at finding herself so quickly transported to the mundane realities of life. 'But I have no fear – I love you. Is there anything in the whole world that could sadden me, other than you? I don't ask you to tell me your secrets. Go and return quickly, because I shall be counting the minutes of your absence.'

The viscount pressed the young woman tenderly to his chest and said,

'I love you, we shall soon be reunited.'

Two days later, he boarded a train and in three days' time he had arrived at the ancient manor of Saski, one of those feudal estates, of which there are thousands in Poland. Perched on a mountain-top, like a gigantic eagle's eyrie, the castle dominated the valley and the vast plains planted with fir-trees as far as the eye could see. The estate was very impressive and the lady of the manor, Miss Athene Saska, no less so. It was said that, in her youth, her life had not been without storms.

She had suffered a disappointment and, wounded in her heart as well as her pride, had fled to the heights of Saski, vowing life-long hatred of marriage and of the male sex. She allowed no man to cross her threshold, except her brother, Gaston's father, and Gaston himself, who was then a baby.

After her brother had died, she concentrated all her ambitions on her nephew, whom she swore to make one of the richest lords of her country. She adopted a life-style which was almost monastic in its simplicity and every year accumulated the revenues from her estates, never selling any part of them until her nephew, now grown-up, began to show that he had all his teeth and a healthy appetite.

'Thirty thousand francs with which I shall supplement the thirty thousand of the viscount's own, inherited from his parents, will allow him to live on a generous scale,' she thought and never once departed from this arrangement.

The old spinster would have liked her nephew to settle close to her but he was young, his soul craved gaiety and love; the cavernous rooms of the castle, and the long avenues through dark forests were not the kind of thing to satisfy the aspirations of a twenty-year-old. So, one fine morning, he had willy-nilly got permission to go to Paris and study law. Ah, Paris, the city of intellect, laughter and love! A place with an atmosphere quite different from Saski.

Gaston breathed it in in deep gulps, soaked himself in it, and had not once, during the easy existence he had quickly built up for himself, found burdensome the promise his aunt had demanded from him before his departure, not to marry as long as she lived.

Get married? What an idea! But suddenly fate had

dragged him on to new paths: marriage was immi-
nent. If his aunt did not release him from his promise,
there was bound to be a rift between them, given the
noble Athene's character. Gaston wanted to benefit
from the element of surprise and so arrived unan-
nounced. He noted some symptoms of tenderness on
the old spinster's rigid features, which emboldened
him; so, after the first effusive greetings, he came
straight out with it.

'What good wind has brought you here?' Aunt
Athene had asked.

'The wind of happiness, which is knocking at my
door and which I have come to ask you to let in for
my sake.'

A frown appeared on the old lady's brow.

'If that happiness does not happen to be wearing
petticoats, I shall certainly do so; otherwise, I shall
hold you to your promise.'

'But, Aunt!' he pleaded.

'I have spoken. You know I shall never change my
attitude.'

'So, if I were to ask for your consent to a marriage
on which my happiness, and even my honour, depend,
you would remain implacable?'

'I would remind you that your honour is pledged
to me by the promise you made me and would say to
you: "no, you must wait till my death sets you free –
otherwise . . . " '

'Otherwise?'

' "Expect nothing from me, either now or in the
future, because I shall consider you to be a perjuror."
But we have not come to that point! So, hush, not
another word. If there is a little intrigue afoot, let it
ripen until my journey through this vale of tears is
over. I am eighty and you won't have long to wait.'

Gaston said nothing. Involuntarily, he glanced at

his aunt. She was tall, thin and wrinkled; her hair was the colour of the peaks of the Jungfrau; her yellow teeth showed evidence of many years of use. But she was as straight as a ramrod, walked five miles every day for the good of her health, ate half a chicken or an equivalent quantity of food at every meal, washed down with a full bottle of claret, without experiencing the lightest discomfort and seemed good for a century, at least.

Gaston spent an unhappy week with her and then returned to Paris. What was he to tell Julia? What was he to do?

As soon as he got back, he left his calling card for Madame Briquart, an ingenious way of telling Julia: I am back. When can I see you?

Her reply came quickly. It said, 'At my aunt's, at two o'clock tomorrow.'

The viscount was a little surprised by these few words; it then occurred to him that Julia had found a means of escaping her mentor's supervision or that perhaps she had no intention of letting him burn his boats that day, but the joy of just seeing her would be enough for him. I'll do whatever I have to do: if necessary, I'll explain the whole situation and we shall see, Gaston told himself.

Julia was not, in fact, alone when he arrived and the colonel's lady was extremely gracious; she offered him her small hand in a friendly fashion and said:

'My dear traveller, have you returned happy and contented?'

Julia must have spoken to her, the viscount thought. All the better, half the work is done. Did she tell her everything, I wonder. I don't suppose she did.

The young woman put her heart into the look she gave him as if she meant thus to send it to him, and he responded with a gaze that was no less tender and affectionate.

'No, Madame, I am afraid not,' the viscount said to the old lady. 'I meant on my return to say to you: I adore your niece, my keenest wish is to make her my companion for life and to ensure for her the brilliant life she deserves. The first part of my plan stands, but the second has had to be modified. My aunt would curse me if I married before her death and her curse would mean that I am reduced to the bare necessities of life. Such as it is, I offer all I have to Mademoiselle Julia. She must decide whether she wants, in spite of it all, to entrust to me the care of her happiness.'

'Julia, you have heard the viscount. What do you say?'

'I have a request to make to you, Aunt. Will you let me talk alone to the viscount? I know that etiquette forbids it but you are so indulgent.'

'My dear child, I'll leave the drawing-room to you two for quarter of an hour, after which I shall return to hear your decision.'

Madame Briquart left the room.

When they were alone, Julia and Gaston immediately flew into each others' arms and were fused in a long kiss.

'Gaston!'

'Julia, my love!'

'Do you still love me?' Julia asked, deeply moved.

'With all my heart, my love.'

'Do you swear by whatever is most holy to you that you will always be mine, as I am yours?'

'By the ashes of my mother,' Gaston said, looking very grave and pale.

A sigh of happiness escaped the young woman's breast.

'Well, then, drive away the cloud that darkens your

brow despite yourself. You must not think for a moment that I should wish to sacrifice your position or your material well-being for a lot of empty conventions. If your aunt wants us to wait until her death, so be it.'

'What, apart from each other?'

'Oh, no, not that. We shall be together always. Only we shall wait to consecrate our union until circumstances permit.'

While she was speaking Julia shone with such an aura of love, her eyes were so frank and her spirit so animated that, in spite of her strange words, she could inspire nothing but respect.

'Ah, my beloved. But have you thought of your honour and the false position such an irregular arrangement would put you in?'

'Don't worry about that. Every medal has its reverse. Things would be much worse if, for the sake of the good opinion of people to whom we are indifferent, we had to make do with cramped lodgings or if you – used to living on a grand scale – were forced to watch every penny. Believe me, we shall rise above all such vain and paltry matters and we shall ask nothing of life but the happiness to which our love entitles us.'

'And your aunt, Madame Briquart?'

'What about her?' that lady, who had just come back, asked.

'I'll tell you,' Julia answered, walking towards her with deliberate steps. 'She will remember that she is an intelligent woman, in every way superior to the vulgar mob and she will say to us, "I do not approve but, on the other hand, I dare not blame you, either."'

'You are speaking in riddles I can't understand.'

'My dear Aunt,' Julia went on, kneeling before her,

'will you be my confessor for a moment, as well as Gaston's, and absolve us from the guilt of the distress we are about to cause you? Aunt, you have heard what Gaston has just told us. Well, I don't want his love for me to give him any concern or pain. I have faith in the steadfastness of his love and I give him my hand without waiting for anyone else to bless our union. Later, when Miss Saska has gone . . .'

'Do not think for a moment that I could approve of such an arrangement even tacitly. Don't you see, my child, that the purity of a woman is such a precious thing that it must not lightly be tossed aside? You don't know about life or what the phrase about union of man and wife means. But I know, and it behoves me to warn you in your inexperience. Nor would the viscount want to take advantage of your innocence.'

'I love her,' Gaston said.

'I shall set your mind at rest, dear, good Aunt, by telling you what I would not dare without my arm round his neck and my heart against his. It is this . . . it is : . . that I am his already, not in words but in deed and that I am,' she continued with her head proudly raised, 'not ashamed of it but proud and happy and that I would sooner give up life itself than the bliss I have tasted in his arms.'

Startled, Madame Briquart rose from her chair.

'What are you saying?' she murmured.

'I am saying that I am not presenting to you Viscount Saski, my fiancé, but Gaston Saski, my lover.'

It was as if a thunderbolt had struck Madame Briquart.

'I don't believe it,' she mumbled.

'Madame,' the viscount now said, coming forward in his turn, 'I give you my word as a gentleman that Julia is my wife – in my heart as well as before God

— and that as soon as my aunt's severity ceases to constrain us, our position will be regularised.'

'You will not expect my house and my respectable chaperonage to shield your illicit *amours?*'

'All we ask of you is that in some corner of your heart you should keep a shred of affection for us.'

'I would things had been different. But what can I do?' she murmured. 'What are your immediate plans?'

'To spend a few days making arrangements to prepare, as best I can, a happy existence for Julia. Will you permit me to seek your advice on that?'

'No, you love this crazed child — that is enough. From now on I shall have nothing to do with whatever she may decide. As for you, Sir, I regret to tell you that from now on my door will be barred to you.'

Madame Briquart got up and left the drawing-room with great dignity, but she said to herself: I cannot act any differently, but Julia has behaved like a woman with a heart; she is what I always thought she was — a real wman.

The viscount hugged Julia, kissed her ardently and left, saying,

'Only a few more days apart, my darling wife, and after that we shall never leave each other.'

CHAPTER SIX

'That's all clear then, Dorothy. Have you fully understood and carried out my instructions?'

'Let your Lordship judge himself. I vouch for the competence of Baptiste, the butler, who has engaged an excellent cook. Tomorrow representatives from Worth, Pinga, Virot and Ferry will call to take her Ladyship's orders. Guerlain have sent their perfumes and Tahan their brushes. I shall be there to attend to anything that may crop up.'

'Excellent, Dorothy. I knew all along I could count on you. Now I have to ask you to deal with a small but delicate task, which I hope you will perform with your usual tact.'

'Would Your Lordship explain?'

'Yes. I knew you at Madame Lucie's and appreciated your work there. But your services here will be of quite a different kind.'

'My discretion has never been questioned anywhere.'

'It's not a question of that — I have complete confidence in you — but of respect, not feigned but real respect, for the woman with whom I am going to share my life. For all those coming into contact with her, as indeed for myself, she will be Viscountess Saska, whom family reasons prevent me from presenting openly and I charge you to see to it that

45

no one in the household ever forgets it. Do you understand?'

'Perfectly, and your Lordship will have no grounds for complaint, I am sure.'

When he had inspected the house, he told himself: the main thing appears to have been achieved; when Julia arrives she'll be able to put in the finishing touches.

'Dorothy!'

'Sir?'

'I want you to put on your best bib and tucker and take this letter to the rue d'Assas. You are to ask for Mademoiselle Julia Thorel and not to give it to anybody but her. She will give you an answer.'

'Certainly, Sir. But what if they don't let me in?'

'You must insist. Get yourself a little carton to serve as a pretext.'

Dorothy bowed and withdrew.

This conversation took place in the very pretty dressing-room of a small town house in the rue de Courcelles which the viscount had had furnished in less than forty-eight hours to have it ready to receive Julia.

Such miracles can happen nowhere but in Paris, where they are a daily occurrence.

An hour later, Dorothy was back at the house.

'Her Ladyship,' she said, 'wishes I should return in two hours' time and accompany her to the carriage, so as to avoid comment by the domestic staff.'

'I want you to go back at the appointed hour: I shall be in the brougham just a few houses away . . .'

'Ah, my darling Julia,' he murmured as he went back to his rooms.

At that moment, Julia, kneeling before her aunt, seized her two hands and said to her:

'I love you, who have been a mother to me.

However long we may not see each other, believe me, my heart will always be close to you.'

Madame Briquart realised that the decisive moment was close. Very moved, she took the young woman's head in her hands, covered it with kisses and briskly returned to her room. For a long time she could be heard weeping and then she left for *Les Charmettes*, where she heard that Julia had called the previous day and had been no less affectionate to her sister. In the end, after chatting with her brother-in-law for some time, she had caught the train to Paris with Coralie.

Madame Briquart asked what had passed between George and the fugitive-to-be.

'Lord, Aunt, what do you want me to tell you? At the bottom of my heart I am more of an admirer than a critic of her way of doing things. But for the world and its prejudices, which I haven't the courage to renounce, I should have shouted it to the roof-tops. But for various reasons I had to restrain myself. What I told that loyal sister, when she asked whether henceforth she would have to stop seeing us, was: "We love you too much to banish you from our presence but we can no longer receive you as we have done in the past. This is how things will be: you will come and see us, but we shall send you no official invitations. Florentine will not visit your house, because we shall regard it as solely Viscount Saski's. Apart from that, my dear, you can count on us as in the past." '

'Well said, George.'

'Will you act in the same way?'

'Things are more delicate, as far as I am concerned. I shall not see her except perhaps at *Les Charmettes*, for the time being at any rate.'

'Do you think she will be happy?'

'She will have the happiness of those who like storms; let us hope her ship will stay afloat.'

By the time Madame Briquart got back to the rue d'Assas, Julia had gone.

At about five, Dorothy had returned and got busy stowing the luggage into the cab she had hired. She then escorted Julia to the brougham where Gaston's caressing hands noticed the nervous quiver that had come upon the young woman as a result of leaving the scene of her childhood memories and of life as a chaste young girl.

'At last you are really mine, my darling. Don't hang your head, beloved,' the viscount said, 'because you are not going to cross the threshold of our home as my mistress but as a wife coming to her husband.'

Julia raised her head which had been bent like a flower shaken by the storm.

'I am not bothered by any such feelings,' she said; 'I am moved by regrets at leaving those I love, a little scared of the unknown which is before me, but I do not feel humiliated in the slightest; far from it, Gaston, I am proud of our love and am not in the least tempted to blush for it in anybody's presence. Had it been any different, I would not now be with you.'

Gaston had, as they say, had experience of life but he had never been captivated by a woman of Julia's stamp; this time he felt drawn by all the flames of attraction and admiration, for a woman strong enough to rise above all received ideas and to seek the sum of happiness, that life might give, only in the radiant vision of the love she had glimpsed.

'Here we are, in our home,' the viscount said, as the brougham stopped in the rue de Courcelles.

The footman hurried out to open the front gate and the viscount stretched out his two hands to help his young wife alight.

Then giving Julia his left arm to take, he said affectionately, 'Will *Madame la vicomtesse* permit me to escort her into her house?'

In answer he received a warm squeeze of the hand and Julia crossed the threshold of her new home, on the tapestries of which the pages of her future life were to be inscribed. It was a charming little nest, set between a garden and courtyard, such as people who prefer a comfortable home to emptier satisfactions might find in this part of Paris. The decorations, though improvised, were harmonious and artistic. The interior decorator, who had been in charge of the arrangements, had bought everything needed lock, stock and barrel from a young couple, more enamoured of pleasure than of frugality, who had to rush back to the horrors of Poland to expiate their sins of extravagance. Julia was enchanted with the surroundings, which she found delightfully suitable to her new life. Her own room was a love-nest with upholstered walls with a design of rose-bush branches of different shades against a background of pearl grey, which she thought enchanting. The carpet, with a white ground and covered with flowers, was ankle-deep; her old-fashioned cretonne-lined dressing-room produced cries of admiration. With its large English wash-basins, its comfortable furniture and its big looking-glasses reflecting one another, it was the epitome of luxury and seemed arranged with the express purpose of giving her pleasure.

'I'll leave you, dear Julia, in Dorothy's care; you can have complete confidence in her. We shall meet again in the drawing-room in half an hour.'

The viscount gave his companion a tender kiss, pressed the button of an electric bell and opened the door of the dressing-room, showing Julia a bed-room in oriental style, which formed part of her own private

49

suite. In a few moments, Dorothy had transformed the young woman's appearance. She opened the suitcases and took out a white linen dress, which Julia ordinarily only wore in the evenings; so she was a little surprised to see her maid preparing to dress her in it.

All the same, she was too much of a woman and too shrewd to let her lady's maid see that the choice of this garment – one of her best and intended for *tête-à-tête* dinners with Gaston – astonished her. She sensed around her the atmosphere of an existence which was still unfamiliar to her and she allowed her hair to be dressed in a more elegant way.

Dorothy had cut a few roses from the *jardinières* with which the drawing-room was decorated; she pinned them to the braids of Julia's hair and to the bodice of her white dress, she did something or other to the swell of the skirt which made all the difference to whether one looked well-dressed or not, sprinkled her with a delicious-smelling eau de cologne and, after giving her her handkerchief and her fan, she asked:

'Does your Ladyship know where the drawing-room is?'

'No I don't, Dorothy. I'd be very pleased if you were to show me the way.'

Respectfully, the maid preceded her mistress and led her to a small sanctum lined with tobacco-coloured satin, filled with bibelots and *objets d'art*, where she found the viscount, who had completed his afternoon toilet. Gaston came forward gallantly and led her to a small settee, on which he sat down beside her, and looked at her with eyes of love.

'My darling, how pretty you look. How much I love you,' he whispered in her ear. 'Do you think you will like it here?'

'I would like it anywhere with you,' Julia answered

in her warm and vibrant voice. 'But here everything is so charming and new to me, used as I am to bourgeois life in the rue d'Assas.'

'You'll lead the same life here, only better,' Gaston replied with a laugh. 'Our future is shaped by our beginnings. You will very gently be introduced to our way of living by Dorothy. To begin with, it will seem a little formal to you but that won't last long. As you get more familiar with our way of doing things, you'll be more at your ease.'

This was a clear hint to Julia and she, though she had hitherto lived in a strictly bourgeois environment, was quick to seize it.

'My dear lord and master, we shall do our best.'

'Your Ladyship is served,' Baptiste announced as he flung open the double doors separating the dining-room from the drawing-room.

Gaston stood up, offered his arm to his young wife and led her to her seat opposite his own at the table.

This first dinner *à deux* seemed delightful to Gaston but less so to Julia. The butler, who did not leave them, and the formality, though unpretentious, perturbed her.

So it was with relief that she found herself back in the little drawing-room and heard Gaston say in his musical voice,

'Now that we are alone, let me tell you that I love you.'

Their lips met in a long kiss; blissfully she heard and then spoke those same words, so delightful to those that know them, delicious trifles which are, nevertheless, whole worlds in themselves.

That evening, passers-by in the rue de Courcelles might well have said:

'There is love here. Salute it. Hallelujah! Long live love!'

Their relationship had been established so quickly that, in spite of the bonds between them, there were a good many intimate pages in the book of their lives that had not yet been read. The outpourings of two creatures who adore each other and delight in conveying to each other their respective impressions is wonderful to behold.

'Darling, will you ask Dorothy to serve tea in your room?' Gaston asked.

'Yes, it's eleven o'clock already.'

Although it was autumn, the evenings were cool. Dorothy had lit a small fire, which cheered up the hearth and warmed the air round them, saturated with heady perfumes.

'Madame is a little tired, Dorothy,' the viscount said. 'Will you help her get undressed; after that we shan't be needing you any more tonight.'

The little table was laid and covered with pastry; the samovar was chirping like a cricket. Julia went into her dressing-room and delivered herself into the hands of her maid, who at once took off all her mistress's clothes, rubbed her from head to toe with a flannel glove impregnated with scented powder, prepared for her some eau de cologne intended for intimate hygiene, handed her an ample night-dress of fine cambric, open from top to bottom and fastened at intervals with pink bows, over which she was to wear a long negligé of white cashmere, lined with pale rose satin. Her stockings were discarded with the rest of what she had worn at dinner; they were replaced with white satin slippers, lined and edged with fur. Her unbraided hair fell half-way down to her shoulders.

Julia had to admit that these efforts had made her look much prettier and that Dorothy had the knack of making her mistresses look charming. That was the viscount's opinion, as well, but he said nothing. He, too, was in a dressing-gown and sat his young wife on his knee, where both drank tea from the same cup and took turns to bite into the same piece of pastry.

It was mad. It was marvellous. But the appetite battens by what it feeds on. So the table was pushed into a corner, the bed beckoned with outstretched arms, the negligé became undone and fell on to the carpet, some of the pink ribbons had to confess themselves powerless to prevent the pieces of diaphanous material they were charged with holding together from parting, the young woman's splendid hidden charms were revealed to her husband, who – having looked – now wanted to devour.

'Julia, I have never seen anything as lovely as you. The woman we love is always the most beautiful in our eyes. This time I shall not be brutal; our embrace will not be painful for either of us, oh, my beloved wife.'

One of her breasts had half escaped from the white fur surrounding it and raised its little head, avid for pleasure. Delicately, Gaston seized it between his fiery lips and rolled it gently. Julia writhed with lubricity under this intoxicating caress. With one encroaching hand, he stroked the small of her back, advanced to her mount of Venus and gently descended its slopes; finally he seized the thighs of his young wife in both hands, parted them and moved his avid tongue about the purple contours of the temple of love and nibbled the quivering tufts of jet surrounding it. He then glued his lips on to the provocative tiny hillock which came towards him, swelling like an angry jay. He seized it in a long kiss of the kind that sometimes kills women but is alone capable of giving them the supreme sensation of earthly voluptuousness.

Julia, under the influence of this fiery caress,

quickly lost consciousness of all else around her; her senses, already awakened by the scene at Madame Briquart's, were not this time distracted by pain and vibrated in unison with Gaston's. When, seeing her gasping and quite crazed, he plunged into her loins with the deliberate pace which makes it possible to savour sensation to the full, she let out a cry the echo of which resounded in the very depths of his heart and fully accorded with what he himself felt. Their beings fused in an unprecedented spasm, the violence of which did not separate them. Their lips became pale and inert, their throats could not utter a sound, their nerves were exhausted. When a sense of reality returned to them, they found themselves in each other's arms. Only those who do not know how to love properly, or to love at all, separate when the satisfaction of physical joy is completed. This was not the case with Julia and Gaston.

The next day, in spite of her discretion, Dorothy could not help noticing when she brought in the hot chocolate that the young couple looked tired. So, when she devised the day's menu to submit to her Ladyship for her approval, she took care to include underdone fillet steak and an old Saint-Estèphe, the virtues of which were well known to her.

CHAPTER SEVEN

Julia had scarcely been in the house in the rue de Courcelles for six weeks but great changes in her way of life had already occurred.

To avoid a false situation, which would make all normal social relationships impossible, Gaston asked her to take the pseudonym of Viscountess Saniska (ostensibly living apart from him), and introduced her to all his friends as such, telling them the romantic story of the young viscountess who had inspired great passion in her young husband, whom she followed to Poland, where the unfortunate viscount, after ten months of happiness, passed away. His young widow, lacking the courage to confine herself in perpetuity to the steppes and forests of Poland, the tracks of which seemed to her less attractive than the avenues in the Bois de Boulogne, came back to her own country and to Paris to seek there the pleasures her youth demanded.

He subsequently introduced her to an old friend of his, the Baroness de Sambreval, to whom he told her true story in confidence and who promised she would introduce the young woman to the world that would henceforth be hers – a cheerful and pleasant world, where intelligence and wit reigned supreme and which was bounded, at one end, by the nobility and the austere *haute bourgeoisie* and, on the other, by the *demi-monde*.

Julia raised some objections because she was afraid she would meet with disapproval, but Gaston dismissed them with a laugh.

'Don't worry, my sweetheart, Parisian society is made up of good sorts, who won't forgive you if you force your shameful secrets upon them but who are not in the least inquisitive. No one will ask you which *arrondissement* you got married in; all you need do is to keep up appearances. Madame de Sambreval is the most tolerant of Parisian old ladies; which is only right because it is those without sin who have the right to cast the first stone.'

'Has she sinned?'

'They say she still does . . . But that's no concern of ours.'

'Gaston, I'd sooner see nobody, if a circle of acquaintances is liable to estrange us from each other.'

'On the contrary, my love, we shall be all the happier to get back to our little nest after being wearied by a little worldly chit-chat.'

'I shall do just as you wish, my beloved, because you are my good genie and I love you for your love, your delicacy and your foresight, for all you do to ensure my happiness, which is vulnerable only on one point.'

'And which is that?'

'The constancy of your affection.'

'In that case, my child, go in peace and sin no more.'

'Never?' the young woman asked with a laugh.

'With anyone but your lord, who is not your master.'

'Oh, but he is, the adored master of my heart, my life and all my being.'

'We'll put that to the test.'

The meal, during which this conversation took place, was nearing its end. Pierre had served coffee and retired discreetly and would not reappear unless called. The viscount rose from the table with a laugh, seized Julia by the waist, made her stand up and then, pushing her in front of him, led her, in spite of her protests, towards a divan on which he deposited her on her knees with her head buried in the cushions.

'Stay there,' he ordered, 'I am the master.'

With an expert hand, he turned up her skirts as you would those of a little girl about to be spanked. The soft folds of her dress fell about her head like a cloche.

'Don't move: I am the master.'

The bottom of the slip joined the skirts and two charming rotundities emerged from billows of cambric and lace.

Gaston then tore a long fringe of silk off the divan and set about punishing her with it as one would a child; only the pink furrows, which usually result from such an action, did not appear; the strokes were administered so gently and so accurately that they produced nothing more than a voluptuous tickling sensation, which was frequently interrupted with passionate kisses. Julia tried to get up but a firm hand restrained her and a deep voice said:

'Mademoiselle, am I the master or not? Have I not the right to chastise you at my pleasure?'

And so the chastisement continued until Gaston's passion got the better of him and he let the garment protecting his fleshy parts slide over his thighs, climbed on to the divan, spread himself over Julia's body and made her understand, by transpiercing her with all his ardour, that if love has only one note at its service, it nevertheless has a lot of different ways of playing it.

The present one was new and seemed to him not a badly chosen one; after a copious ejaculation, there was silence.

Julia did not move.

'Are you dead, my darling?' he asked at last.

'No, no, on the contrary . . .'

'The devil, it looks as if you liked that. In that case – repay me for the correction you have just received in the same coin. After all, I deserve it.'

In one bound, the young woman stood up and Gaston's dressing-gown fell on to the floor; he, himself, was bent over the divan with his night-shirt lifted up by Julia's right arm; it was the dainty hands of this new type of little mother which first thrashed him and then kissed him. Below the cleft of his buttocks, the little apples of love appeared. The young woman, in whipping him, lightly stroked them so that they swelled up again with their intoxicating liquor; she lowered herself and seized them between her red lips; she rolled them in her mouth, covered them with her hot saliva and seemed never to want to stop when Gaston turned round briskly, threw her on her back, seized her legs, put them round his own body like a belt and, kneeling in front of her at the level of her love grotto, voluptuously plunged into her, at the same time pointing to a large looking glass in front of them.

'Have a look,' he said.

She saw the exquisite, regular, gentle to and fro movement of the instrument of love which she found exquisite.

Deliciously excited, Julia with a charming gesture tore off the fastenings of her bodice and her breasts, like those of a goddess of love, appeared, trembling with passion and voluptuousness. Gaston let his caressingly agile finger play with the little pink buttons which were wantonly raising their little heads.

'Oh, Gaston, my love, I feel I am dying, dying of happiness.'

'Me, too, my darling. Ah, I have come. It's all for you.'

A double cry of supreme ecstasy escaped the lips of the entangled couple and the divan received the amorous baptism which it had missed before. A few hours later, Baptiste asked Dorothy for a certain cleaning fluid of which the lady's maid had a supply and the two servants exchanged a meaningful smile as they got busy removing the stains from the divan. At that time, Gaston and Julia were at the baroness's to whose Tuesday 'At Homes' they had been invited, and then went for a stroll in the woods until dinnertime when they returned home. They were a little tired from the morning's exertions but happy and loving; they thought everyone who claimed the earth was not a place of utter delight, complete fools.

At the same time, the baroness said to her old friend, General Don José de Corriero,

'I assure you she is absolutely delicious and deserves to have roses strewn in her path.'

'Tut,' he replied. 'You are letting yourself get carried away.'

'You'll see.'

'Yes, I'll see and, if I can, I'll touch.'

'I forbid you to.'

'Still jealous, Louise?'

'Yes.'

'Let's not go on like this. What if we were overheard?'

'People would be foolish enough to make fun of us,

obviously. Still, does the heart have to grow old when the hair on one's head goes white?'

'This subject would lead us a long way; you know that I love you, as I know that you love me. But all we can do about it these days is to cherish our memories, if we don't want to seem ridiculous to the world.'

'Amen,' the baroness replied.

Gaston's friends were received at Viscountess Saniska's house every Thursday and the following Tuesday she was due to attend Baroness Sambreval's At Home.

The old lady had a sumptuous apartment on the first floor of a fine house on the Boulevard Saint-Michel done up in autumnal colours – but of an autumn that still remembered the summer.

Sitting in her small drawing-room, which was lined with *feuilles mortes* silk, surrounded by thousands of bibelots reminding her of her brilliant youth, she awaited her guests, who soon started to arrive, one after the other.

At about eleven o'clock, Julia, the viscount and one of his friends, Hector Vaudreuil, a brilliant senior army officer, who could not grasp that his twenties had long ago flown away, made their appearance.

Dorothy had surpassed herself on this occasion and Julia's appearance, ravishing and in excellent taste, testified to her lady's maid's talents. Over a rose-petal coloured satin sheath dress, she had amassed billows of tulle, in the delicious confusion of which, there nestled bunches of Bengal roses – the hearts of which, artistically arranged, decorated her hair.

The young woman's arms, bare of all jewellery, were displayed in all their breath-taking beauty under the light of the chandeliers. A murmur of admiration made itself heard as she walked up to the hostess to pay her respects.

The baroness introduced several guests to her, as is the custom. Don José treated her like the star of the party. More and more, the young woman, adulated and surrounded by admirers, felt that if this was a dream of life it was an enchanting one from which she never wanted to wake.

By the time she left the baroness's flat, she had given several of the gentlemen permission to call on her and agreed to visit some of the ladies, in short she had become part of the world in which one was expected to shine. To do so, it was not enough to be favoured by fortune − you had to be a somebody on the strength of your wit, your beauty or both. A somebody accepted by that world, which does not always take the path leading to heaven but in which there is a good deal of amusement and, by my troth, turns out, on closer inspection, to be a good deal more desirable than one that has nothing to offer but tedium.

CHAPTER EIGHT

Time went on its way, as it is wont to do, and took its toll of all the figures in our story.

At *Les Charmettes*, too, its influence was felt. George Vaudrez went on adoring his wife but his cheeks were horribly sunken and his hands, which were afflicted by a constant tremor, showed he was suffering from nervous debility, which required medical attention.

'Good grief,' his friend Albert said to him from time to time when he saw him in Paris, 'you mustn't take my rejuvenating drops so often. They were all right for the wedding night but, as a regular thing, they're pretty dangerous.'

'What can I do?' George replied. 'My wife is charming but still waters run very deep. My spirit is very willing but it's a certainty that my flesh is weak.'

'Indeed it is. I guarantee if you don't have six weeks' rest at some spa or other, you'll be a goner.'

Poor George! Deep down inside, he knew how much truth there was in such a prophecy. But how could he make up his mind to leave Florentine? If he took her with him, good-bye to the cure! He might as well stay at home and not exacerbate the situation by the strain of a journey.

As for Florentine, she had no complaints about her intimate sensations and, had George but known it, he could easily have saved himself a lot of trouble and exhaustion. His young wife did not sufficiently appreciate his efforts and infinitely preferred the preliminary caresses with which he would accompany it to the final consummation. In this, he faithfully followed the precept that bids husbands and lovers never to omit ringing the bell before entering the house.

Under the caresses of George's expert finger, she experienced ineffable pleasures, greatly superior to those she obtained from full union with her consort. Had she dared to confess this, a great load would have been taken off George's mind, but she was afraid of hurting his feelings. But there was one black cloud in the blue sky of her existence: she had been married six months and there were still no indications of any hope of motherhood. This was the cause of the caresses she heaped, and the demands she made, on George. Aunt Briquart smiled when she heard Florentine's confidences.

Meanwhile, spring had passed and summer was nearing its end. Florentine underwent the influence of the flowering of nature and George's tremor got worse and worse.

'My dear Vaudrez,' his doctor said to him one day, having come to *Les Charmettes* for lunch, 'we are too good friends for me not to tell you the truth, so here it is: if you don't leave for the seaside as soon as possible, I give you no more than six months of good health; complete collapse is knocking at the door.'

'You are joking, doctor. And what about my wife?'

'My good friend, she will have to go where she pleases; but I must tell you that she is one of the prime causes of your trouble that need to be eliminated. You must be away from her for a month or six weeks, at the very least. There's no use beating about the bush. Do you understand me?'

'Perfectly. It's sad not to be twenty any longer.'

'I tell myself that every day,' the doctor replied with a laugh.

'But Florentine is still in her twenties – the only one of us who is.'

'What's happening to Aunt Briquart?'

'She can come and spend the period of my absence in the country. But she claims that being surrounded by woods gives her rheumatism, that the air round here is humid, that there are mosquitoes, toads and goodness knows what else.'

'So! The colonel's lady has no taste for rural life. Well, then, let's fix things up accordingly. You can send the ladies to Saint-Gildas in Brittany. There is a holiday home there on the shores of the Atlantic, run by nuns on the very site of the monastery which Abélard, after his misadventure, wanted to reform. Evidently this was an enterprise full of danger, because the Mother Superior at Saint-Gildas never fails to show visitors the skylight of the cell from which he escaped the fury of his monks, who – having in vain uttered the threats which later inspired the author of the fable *The Fox who Had His Tail Cut Off* – tried to get rid of their embarrassing abbot by poisoning him.'

'And no men are allowed?'

'No, they only have families. The husbands, themselves, are made to stay in the village. You need not worry in the slightest.'

'I am not jealous, but . . .'

'Yes, I understand . . . but you can send them there and have complete peace of mind.'

In the evening of the day after this conversation, George praised Saint-Gildas so highly to Florentine and Madame Briquart, that he fired them with great enthusiasm for a holiday on the Rhuis peninsula. A fortnight later the ladies alighted outside the massive great gate of the convent and took possession of the monastic cells allocated to them – their spirits slightly daunted by the primitive simplicity of the place.

The aunt pouted slightly, but the young woman seemed charmed by the kind of life that was led in that neck of the woods.

The following morning, she went out to explore the beach, taking particular pleasure in sinking her feet in the sand and shrimping. The shrimps, here called *berniques* were prised off the rocks and eaten live. After a few days, these innocent pleasures had made her much more lively.

They witnessed the arrival with great to-do at the convent of the Duchess d'Hérisez and her son Gaétan, a handsome adolescent of eighteen, whose chin was covered with no more than a slight down and whose peaches-and-cream complexion and innocent blue eyes did not in the slightest 'suggest manhood', as the old nuns said in a whisper. He looked like a cherub, though he had passed the age above which members of the stronger sex were banned from the convent. But in this case, the rules were not too strictly interpreted: the duchess, a pillar of the league of patrons of the community, had declared that Gaétan had only just had his fifteenth birthday and nobody dared question her on this point.

It took very little time before he became Florentine's constant companion on her beach walks. Madame Briquart and the duchess raised no objections and so the children, as they were called in the convent, were allowed to wander about in peace. Naturally, Cherub fell madly in love with his companion and became, in his imagination, the greatest scoundrel in the world. But he was shy and said nothing about his passionate desires, which were reflected only in the expression of his eyes.

Florentine enjoyed her youthful admirer's passion very much and for a month they had been flirting away in a way that would make Yankees, even the most accomplished in this art, green with envy. Meanwhile, Madame Briquart, who was bored to death, had the idea of going off to Paris for a week on the pretext of consulting her doctor in the capital.

'I'll be back long before George finishes his cure; for the rest, I'll leave you in the care of the duchess, so what more could you ask?'

No objections were raised. She had been at her ease at home in the rue d'Assas for four days, when one morning a telegram from George arrived at Saint-Gildas, saying:

'Planning to spend winter at Menton. Join me there forthwith.'

'What should I do?' Florentine asked the duchess, quite startled by the news.

'My dear child, you are too young to travel alone. You need a chaperon. You can have Gaétan.'

'Cherub?'

'Precisely. He is old enough to look after you on the journey but young enough not to compromise you. Will you accept him as a travelling companion?'

'If you find it convenient, I would, with pleasure.'

'Well, that's agreed then. Wire your lord and master that you are coming. You can pick up your aunt in Paris. She won't be distressed at not seeing the beaches of Saint-Gildas again, and you can resume your journey the following day.'

The climate of Brittany has its charms particularly for those who love grey skies, but it also has its disadvantages, the first and foremost of which is its highly capricious nature. The weather was still fine when George's wire arrived. When they left, the wind was raging amongst the cliffs and the cries of the seagulls announced bad weather.

Gaétan had received detailed lessons from his mother about how a gentleman should comport himself when a lady does him the honour of accepting his company. As Florentine took much pleasure in allowing herself to be spoilt by him and treated him like a child of no consequence, Cherub took a great many liberties and nobody took any notice of the snow which had begun to fall relentlessly. As far as Nantes, everything went well, but from there on, it was noticed that the train proceeded at a snail's pace, though this did not unduly upset our two travellers. Gaétan had wrapped Florentine up well; he snuggled up close to her under the blanket and the cold weather did not seem to bother them too much. All the same, there were frequent stops.

By the time they arrived at Le Mans, they were two hours late and the station-master appeared, to announce to the travellers that they could not go on beyond La Lupe, because the line was blocked.

Things were getting serious and Florentine stopped laughing. She found her companion was less of a child than she thought and the prospect of being delayed for the whole of a night did not appeal to her; in fact, she was rather frightened. Suddenly the train stopped before Bretoncelles. Half an hour went by and it did not budge.

'Oh, God, my little Gaétan, what's to become of us?'

They had adopted the ways of childhood at Saint-Gildas, Gaétan addressed her as *Madame* but the young woman, who was less formal, merely called him *Gaétan* or *Cherub*.

It was perishingly cold and there were only two things to do: send wires to reassure the family and go and find lodgings. This is what they set about doing amid laughter, when the first shock had passed. There were two feet of snow. How were they to get to Bretoncelles, their haven of refuge, where they were in danger of having to spend three or four days and which, from the point of view of distractions, had much less to offer than Paris?

'Madame, I shall be your horse,' Gaétan said with a deep blush.

'What do you mean?'

'You can't walk in this snow; you must get up on my shoulders and I shall carry you piggy-back.'

Now it was Florentine's turn to blush.

'I'm being silly,' she told herself, 'he's just a child.' So she climbed up and sat astride his shoulders.

It does not help being beardless. When you have a young woman with whom you are in love on your shoulders, it is bound to excite you, so that by the time they reached their lodgings, Gaétan was quite wrought up.

Their peasant hosts, sensing a windfall, took great care to warm the travellers and to prepare their supper. The unforeseen situation and the comfortable warmth which now surrounded them revived the young woman. Both were very happy in each other's company and did justice to the cabbage soup, bacon and white wine with which they were served.

At half past nine they were warming themselves by the fire, chatting about this and that. Behind all this, the little, wicked God of love was hidden, laughing in the wings. Florentine thought that her husband, who believed her to be in the care of the colonel's lady, would hardly be pleased if he saw her enjoying herself in Cherub's company, as she was doing.

'He's only a child, after all,' she told herself, to still the voice of conscience.

Suddenly a deep voice interrupted them.

'*Monsieur, 'dame*, your room is ready; you may go up any time. There's a fine bed and plenty of blankets, though when young people like you touch they don't feel the cold any more.'

These simple words confounded Florentine and greatly moved Gaétan, who nevertheless kept his head and whispered to his companion.

'Don't put him wise and don't be afraid. After all, I *am* a gentleman.'

'Just a kid,' she thought.

All the same, a secret emotion seized her.

'If we undeceive him,' Gaétan went on, 'he'll throw us out and that won't be funny.'

That was true. Florentine understood, and followed him without protest. When they arrived in the room they looked at each other and laughed.

'Well?' she asked.

'Well, you are going to take the bed and I shall spend the night in the kitchen.'

'Oh, no, I'd be much too frightened all alone! Go out for a moment and then come back.'

After about half an hour, Gaétan came back, looking very pale. He stared boldly, and with curiosity, at the bed in which lay Florentine, her fine blonde head on the pillows and her lovely body outlined under the sheets and blankets.

Gaétan felt a tremor pass through him – ideas, which his mother had never inculcated into him, began to seethe in his head.

'No,' he told himself; 'she is under my care. I must not exploit the situation. All the same . . .'

He sat down on a chair, the least uncomfortable he could find, adopting the attitude of a faithful dog lying at his mistress's feet. After a quarter of an hour, his teeth were chattering and he was in danger of turning into an icicle.

Florentine took pity on him.

'Oh dear,' she said. '*Honi soit qui mal y pense.* Little Cherub, you're going to catch your death of cold. Come and lie beside me with all your clothes on.'

Gaétan thought he would faint when he heard this charming invitation.

'Well, what are you waiting for?' Madame Vaudrez asked.

'I am frozen.'

'Go and get a hot water bottle and warm yourself up.'

It did not take him long to find one and with chaste precautions he slid it under the feet of the young woman, which he saw emerge from the bed-clothes all pink and white; then he buttoned up his greatcoat, lay down and looked at his neighbour who laughed in his face.

'Gosh, Cherub, if my husband saw us, what would he say?'

'He would probably react in a way we'd both find disagreeable.'

'And yet . . .'

'Yes, yes,' Gaétan mumbled. In spite of the freezing cold outside, he felt hot.

Neither of them was anxious to go to sleep, so they talked – so well, that Gaétan's heart flowed over and he dared to say to Florentine as he embraced her,

'I am drawn to you by an irresistible force. I can't bear it any longer. I love you.'

'Come, come, you baby,' Florentine answered in a slightly mocking tone of voice.

'I may be a baby but, in this case, a baby that wants to return to his little mother's womb.'

'And what about my husband?'

Poor Cherub! Beads of sweat formed on his forehead, the wings of his pink nostrils, like those of a young girl, trembled strangely.

Florentine was so pretty! Gaétan was new to the game. The orange blossom, without actually being profaned, might easily have crowned him but there are things one knows, probably instinctively, because suddenly his neighbour cried out,

'Stop that, Gaétan, you're tickling.' But Gaétan was disobedient.

'What is the meaning of this?'

'The meaning is that I adore you.'

'What does it prove?'

'That I want to owe to you my first sensation of love.'

'Your virginity? You are making me a present of it? That's sweet of you. But is it true that you have never . . . ? Tell me your intimate life story.'

'I have never approached a woman as I am approaching you. My tutor or my mother never left me out of their sight for a moment.'

'How strange. All the same, now that you have made your declaration I can't go on holding you in my arms. You're going to freeze, but that's your fault! You ought to have been good, and what you are doing now is very bad indeed, Monsieur Cherub. Fie, you're doing it to a married woman, which is very reprehensible.'

'No, it is very nice and I want you.'

'Go away, you little devil.'

Florentine pushed him out of bed, but her action must have been poorly co-ordinated because, though it was intended to force the delinquent off the top of the bed, he found himself in it, instead.

'You naughty boy, you're as crafty as a monkey. Gaétan, be good or I'll send you away for good.'

The child obeyed but, like so many other children, he was never as naughty as when you could not hear or see what he was doing. He was, in fact, busy unbuttoning his trousers.

Suddenly, Florentine gave a little cry.

'So you're starting your nonsense again. Baby, I am getting quite vexed. The idea of your virginity is quite appealing and if I were not an honest woman, we might see. But I love my husband. The bad boy, he won't listen to me. You're tickling me, Gaétan, I'll tell your mother on you.'

But Gaétan went on tickling and a nervous laugh seized the young woman and then stopped as if stifled.

Cherub took advantage of this lull and Florentine could only protest against the gift of that flower of love which her companion insisted on giving her; he was imposing it upon her but, it must be admitted, her own senses made themselves into accomplices of Cherub's efforts.

She noticed an appreciable difference between what she was feeling and what she knew to be right; gradually, she stopped defending herself and the happy Baby was forgiven.

Once . . . twice . . . even a third time. Suddenly a flash of insight came to Florentine, who told herself:

'Now I know why I shall probably never have children by George. In this world it is only faith which is the saving grace. Let us keep his faith intact and make him happy without his participation.'

To make her beloved husband happy, Florentine heaped blessings on Cherub, who asked no more than to show himself lavish with his demonstrations of love, so the night was well employed.

Laughingly, Gaétan and Florentine presented themselves to Madame Briquart next day. She was full of thanks to Gaétan, who was a little embarrassed at accepting them.

'Don't flatter him like that, Aunt,' the young woman said. 'He does not deserve your exaggerated praises.'

'Ah, Madame.'

'All right, all right, you little devil, we understand each other.'

Florentine, accompanied by her aunt, joined her husband and, six weeks later, the doctor told Monsieur Vaudrez, who was concerned about a minor ailment of his wife's:

'It is not very serious. In a few months' time, the final crisis will result in the birth of a fine baby.'

'Do you think so, doctor?'

'No, I don't *think* so, I *know!* You are still a vigorous lover, and I wish you a son.'

George, who was in his seventh heaven, warmly embraced his young wife. She blushed deeply, no doubt out of happiness and deep emotion.

CHAPTER NINE

While George was taking care of his health and
Florentine was staying in the Rhuis peninsula, the
Saki-Saniska household was on its travels, too. They
had toured Spain, seen Madrid and the Manolas, the
arid Mancanares, the ruins of old Iberia and Barce-
lona, when they felt the need for a period in Saint-
Jean-de-Luz, where the two of them had now been
resting for a week without yet thinking too much
about returning to Paris.

They still loved each other very much, though
occasionally little black clouds of jealousy were beginning to mar the bright azure sky of the young woman's
love.

If these Poles were the most charming knights of
love one could hope to meet, they were also very light-
winged butterflies which liked to flutter from flower
to flower – so Julia sometimes mused sadly.

That day was intolerably hot, although it was close
to the end of autumn. A strenuous excursion had
added to the exhaustion of this normally very robust
daughter of Eve. So, after dinner, Julia told Gaston
she wanted to retire, leaving him free to spend the
evening with his friends, an offer he accepted with
alacrity. The young woman intended to go to bed and
sleep but only the first part of her plan was achieved.

It is said, 'What can you do alone in a bed when you can't sleep? Muse.' And that is what she did.

Whether it was the buzzing of the mosquitoes round her that irritated her nerves or whether it was the memory of the incidents of the day going round her head that disturbed her, the hours went by without Morpheus scattering his soothing poppies over her.

'Why,' Julia asked herself, 'did he exchange glances with that blonde who arrived yesterday? I should have thought nothing of it, if he had simply told me the facts. After all, there's nothing remarkable about his knowing her before he met me. But no, he denies it. He is lying. Why?'

Her imagination became worked up.

'I love him too much and let him see it too clearly,' she decided. 'From now on, I'll pretend to be cool.' She looked at her watch. 'Two o'clock in the morning. Where can he be?'

She heard a sound, not of boots but of soft pumps, coming up the stairs.

'Oh, he's coming, expecting me to receive him with open arms and to scold him sweetly with tender kisses in between. Well, he'll have to think again. I shall pretend to be asleep, however hard he tries to wake me.'

And the young woman turned towards the wall. Soon the door turned on its creaking hinges and slightly hesitant steps were heard on the carpet.

'Good,' Julia said to herself. 'He will have had supper, be a bit tiddly and want his oats. I can tell by his footsteps. Ordinarily, he would make a bit more noise. Still, I shan't say a word.'

A few moments later, Julia heard him trying to light a candle. He lit a match but it went out.

'Damn it, I haven't got any more,' he murmured. His voice sounded a bit strange to Julia.

'The party must have been good,' Julia thought.

He decided to do without illumination, took off his shoes and trousers and slid into bed. He gave a little start when he found it was occupied.

'Can it be that the blonde, who made eyes at me all afternoon, is here to give me a surprise. What a happy rogue that would make me!'

His caressing hands roamed round her body next to his.

'Do what you like,' Julia, who believed it was Gaston beside her, said to herself, 'I can feel you but I am sulking, so you might as well stop.'

She soliloquised in silence but her neighbour acted as if he had heard her.

'Let's go,' he said under his breath, as well, 'we'll have her in her feigned sleep; that'll save the comedy of false modesty. It would be uncouth of me not to play along with the whim of a pretty woman – she can't be anyone but my blonde apparition.'

Delicately and discreetly, George put his hands round the waist next to him, slipped lower into bed, introduced himself into the sanctuary of happiness and prepared to avail himself on a grand scale of the hospitality being offered him.

At that moment, Julia had a secret feeling.

'That's strange,' she thought, 'could it be the champagne? It is supposed to be treacherous to a degree; I have never known Gaston like this; this is not at all pleasant and I shall forbid him in future to drink the Widow Cliquot's products. Luckily, I have decided to sulk. He is making that quite easy for me.'

George was beavering away with perseverance; and it is well known that the practice of this virtue rarely fails to lead to success.

Suddenly, the good fellow, who was having marvellous sensations, produced a meaningful whinnying sort of noise, which was greeted with an exclamation of horror.

'Oh, my God, it isn't Gaston! Who is it? Help!'

'It's all right, my little friend, there is no point in your shouting. I am a gentleman and I know how to behave with ladies. Besides it's too late now. We'll try to light a candle and then make our explanations like sensible people. I flirted with you all afternoon and now I find you in my bed. I was delighted. This is just the result I had hoped for, though I confess that I did not expect it quite so soon. However that may be, I find you most desirable and I am overjoyed at having got to know you.'

There was no answer.

George managed to find a match which worked; candlelight illuminated the room; he looked at the bed but all he could see was bed-clothes.

'Come, come, my lovely child, what you are doing is senseless. Why should we stand on ceremony with each other? I warn you: I won't have it.'

His bed-mate reacted with complete silence.

George crossly looked round the room; he saw the colours of the curtains were different from those in the room he had been given earlier that evening. Quickly he tore off the blanket and laid bare the ravishing head of a woman, the sight of which completely bowled him over.

'Julia!'

'George! Oh, my God!' the woman murmured.

'Good Lord,' George managed to say, 'we've just done a foolish thing – a very foolish one.'

'George, I had no idea,' Julia said in a barely audible voice.

'I am certain of that, my dear child. Good grief, I went into the wrong room. So you took me for the viscount?'

'Yes, I was vexed because he was coming back so late.'

'Poor Saski. We've just unwittingly illustrated the saying: "he who yields his place loses it."'

'Oh, no,' Julia exclaimed, 'he has lost nothing and I'd gladly give up ten years of my life for what has just occurred not to have happened.'

'I am less distressed than you, my lovely sister-in-law, you are charming and . . .'

'What about Florentine?' Julia asked in a severe tone.

'She shall know nothing, because I presume you share my determination to observe complete discretion about this episode.'

'Certainly.'

'What a coincidence! Have you been here for some time?'

'Yes, we stopped at Saint-Jean-de-Luz for a rest. And you, what are you doing here all alone?'

'I came to see a friend and in a few days' time must go on to Biarritz, where Florentine will join me. But, my child, it is not wise to go on chatting here. If your viscount should come in and find me as scantily dressed as you, at this hour, and in your bedroom, he might take it amiss and not believe that we are together merely as a result of my having mistaken the door, so I'll make off.'

George hurriedly got dressed, pecked Julia fraternally on the forehead and sought his own room.

It was none too soon. The young woman had scarcely had time to remove the evidence of her involuntary transgression when Gaston came in.

Quite naturally, to cover up her confusion, the viscountess made him a scene about the late hour of his return. There was a quarrel and a reconciliation – all this took time.

The walls of hotel rooms are very thin; this made it impossible for George to get to sleep, so he fell to thinking about the situation. He came to a wise decision: next morning, by the very first train, he left for Biarritz and sent Florentine the wire which made her leave Saint-Gildas so precipitately.

Let no-one deny the power of destiny.

If chance had not made George take a trip to Saint-Jean-de-Luz, or made him mistake his bedroom door, he would not have made his wife leave Brittany so suddenly. Gaétan would not have accompanied her and the senior branch of the Vaudrez family would have become extinct for want of issue.

CHAPTER TEN

Travelling is a delightful pastime but, however enthusiastically one may have admired the wonders scattered over the four corners of the globe, this does not detract from the relief one feels when Paris once again appears on the horizon. Paris, the town of laughter and of love, of wise men and of fools, the only place where, whoever you are or whatever place on the social scale you occupy, you are sure to find a group just like you.

The little house in the rue de Courcelles had a festive air for its mistress's homecoming. Dorothy had sent a wire to Baptiste, who had helped her make it as welcoming as possible, and Gaston, as well as Julia, were quite moved when they crossed the threshold of the pretty little bedroom where they had tasted together the delights of their intoxicating pleasures.

He took her in his arms and pressed her close to his chest.

'Are you still mine, darling Gaston, mine alone?', she asked.

'To my dying breath, my love.'

His loving lips, pressed against the young woman's, sealed this promise with the sweetest of seals.

'Alas, in this ocean of ages we can never cast anchor for a single day,' the poet says. This is a sad truth, as sad as that other which says, 'Frailty thy name is woman', though this latter has a more general application and should really read: 'Frailty, thy name is mankind'.

The Saniska-Saskis were caught again in the Parisian social whirl. Gaston, in great demand by his friends and elations, became more niggardly with his attendances at the Saniska house and Julia, in between visits, resuming her At Homes and, in partnership with Don José de Corriero, looking after the Baroness, who was dangerously ill, noticed only that gradually the intimate links between her lover and herself were becoming slacker. She returned home at night so preoccupied that she quite liked getting into bed alone and resting till the morning without any *intermezzo* of love. But all the same, an ill wind was blowing over their love-nest. Gaston still loved her and no feminine influence was at work to lessen the sentiments he felt in his heart for Mademoiselle Thorel (the Viscountess Saniska's real name).

But another terrible rival was gaining ground: his gambling fever, to which he had always been subject but which had been relegated to a subsidiary place when his *liaison* with Julia began. Now that the first flush of this relationship was over, it took the upper hand again and wreaked vengeance for the infidelities by which it had been slighted. Gaston lost enormous sums, without admitting it. He became desperate, tried to recoup his losses and merely succeeded in sinking ever deeper into the morass, as often happens in such cases.

Meanwhile, Julia lost her worldly protector; the baroness breathed her last in her arms and her death-bed wish was that Julia should console her poor Spanish friend, whose devoted and loving arm never failed to stand by her and who now, grief-stricken, was on his knees, weeping, beside her bed, his head hidden in the blankets.

Poor Don José! This death was such a heavy blow that he could not have borne it without the gentle attentions with which Julia now surrounded him.

The baroness's heirs instructed that the pretty apartment on the Boulevard Saint-Michel be sold, but the general could not bear the idea of all those bibelots, nearly all of which recalled an emotion, an incident, a trifle – you might say – but a trifle that assumes enormous importance in the mind of the person who has loved and is left behind to live out his or her life alone. The general could not bear the idea of all these things being scattered to the four winds, so Julia said to him:

'Would you like me to buy our poor baroness's property on your behalf, so that nothing needs to be changed?'

The general was a very wealthy man; he accepted the suggestion enthusiastically and the young woman arranged matters with great skill and diplomacy, exactly as Don José wished.

'On my death,' he said, 'you must become the owner of this treasure. Who would appreciate it better than you?'

Every day, at the precise time that he used to visit his old friend, the general arrived. The drawing-room would have been got ready to receive him and Julia would hold out her hand. The warmth he had felt for Mademoiselle Thorel from the first day he had met her turned into adoration. To him, this young woman was the incarnation of goodness; he came to look upon her with a jealous eye and with all the fervour of a southerner for the Madonna. But he noticed a dark cloud on the pale brow which, in daughterly fashion, was bent towards him every day. He wanted to know the reason for it.

This had been going on for some time, for the young woman's eyes had been opened and she was very worried by Gaston's state. It was not in the boulevard Saint-Michel but in his own home that Don José was able to pursue his investigations into the matter, because early one morning, Viscountess Saniska had herself announced there.

'What is the matter, my child?' he asked, made anxious by this reversal of their normal habits.

'I do not know, dear friend, what the matter is but something terrible is going on. Last night, Gaston came in. He took me in his arms gloomily and then with frenzied rage; he slept fitfully, spoke of death, gaming, dishonour – and I don't know what else – but I am very frightened and beg you to join us for luncheon today.'

'I'll be there as soon as I have got ready.'

'I shall wait for you here.'

Two hours later, when Gaston arrived at the rue de Courcelles for luncheon, he found himself face to face with Don José.

'Here, so early?' he asked with an air of surprise, 'and all alone? Where is Julia?'

'She was weeping while waiting for you and I sent her away to bathe her pretty eyes, which her tears were spoiling . . .'

'Why was she weeping?'

'That's what you are going to tell me. I hope. Be of good cheer, Viscount. Julia cannot be happy unless you are. Well then, it seems some cog in the machinery of your little affairs has gone wrong. If I understand what she said to me correctly – she does not know herself what the matter is – she senses with the intuition of a woman in love that there is some disaster in the air. We are both men of the world: can't we talk about it?'

'It's a simple enough thing. Last night, I lost 150,000 francs, which I haven't got, at cards. I have had a run of bad luck ever since I got back to Paris. If Isaac Kapuski cannot lend me the money before tonight, against a mortgage on the inheritance I am expecting from my aunt, I have no choice but do what you would do in a similar case. I am sure you understand.'

'Perfectly. But have you thought of this? You have no right to put an end to your life as long as Julia is not your wife.'

The viscount shrugged his shoulders.

'Let us not mouth noble sentiments. If Mademoiselle Thorel, whom I love with all my heart, had not become my mistress, she would have become another's. Is this not the fate in this fair land of France, of all women whom the heavens have destined to be born beautiful but poor amidst more prosperous contemporaries?'

'You are no doubt speaking under the influence of the moral fever that has you in its grip; not another word on this score, I beg you. You will regret what you have said as soon as you come to your senses. You owe 150,000 francs, you say. They have to be paid by tomorrow – there's no question of that. Well then, on condition that you make a complete break with the usurer whose name you have just mentioned and that you will not gamble henceforth, I shall have that amount put at your disposal by my lawyer. Here's a note to him.'

'You would do that?'

'I am doing it. Now let us make haste to reassure your dear viscountess, who loves you more than you deserve. In matters of love, women are greatly superior to us.'

'That may well be so.'

As soon as she came in, Julia could see that the skies had brightened.

'I present my penitent to you,' Don José said. 'He has confessed and I absolved him, on condition he obtains your pardon for having made you cry.'

'Making you shed tears, my charming child,' Gaston murmured tenderly, 'will you forgive me for that?'

'What was it all about, I want to know.'

'A debt of honour, darling, but everything has now been fixed up, thanks to our good friend here. Only I must go away to try and move to pity the noble Miss Athene Saska, whose measures of financial retrenchment have lately become worrying.'

'You are going to leave us again?'

'It's the first time since we set up home together.'

'I shall come with you.'

Gaston – with an imperceptible movement of his eyes – drew her attention to the general. He had gone pale and Julia understood that the pursuit of her own happiness must not allow her to forget, at this moment above all, how necessary her presence was to the generous and devoted old man, whom she had promised to surround with the most tender care.

'My dear,' Gaston said out loud, 'the plains of Poland are a sad sight at this time of year. Saski would depress you for three months on end and that would be a pity.'

'You are quite right,' she said and turned to the general. 'You'll have to keep me company; you'll lunch and dine with me and we shall talk about him by the fireside.'

'A fortnight at most, my beloved,' the viscount said 'and I'll be back.'

'Take longer, if you like,' the general said. 'You mustn't worry, I'll take good care of her.'

A few days later a horse-drawn sledge loaded with luggage, through the windows of which could be seen the head of the viscount emerging from a vast number of fur wraps, drew up in front of the outside staircase of the castle and soon afterwards the ancient major-domo solemnly announced Viscount Saski to his mistress.

While this was going on, the driver tidied up the vehicle and smiled as he separated the remnants of a bunch of violets from the fur wraps and picked up a tiny, scented lawn handkerchief, which had embroidered in the corner, instead of initials, the figure of a winged mannikin armed with a bow and arrow.

He wondered what this could mean and whether he ought to return it to the viscount at once or wait until the young master had got to his suite of rooms. He decided on the latter course – a wise decision.

The viscount, true Polish butterfly that he was, could not spend the week that had gone by since his departure from Paris without breathing in the *odor della femina;* so he was lucky enough to find an old girlfriend of his in Warsaw, a pleasant woman, whose first fruits he had plucked, and who, thanks to his generosity, had been able to set herself up in a flower-shop, where she did excellent business.

'Kate, would you like to keep me company during the journey?'

Kate said *yes* and so a comfortable travelling sledge was fixed up, filled with bear and fox skins, on both of which they surrendered to all the delights of a rediscovered and shared voluptuousness, with all the abandon of years ago. These were not the feverish sensations of Paris, for Kate was gentle, loving but not very knowledgeable; her pale complexion, her periwinkle blue eyes, her cool lips, like the flowers that she sold, the scent of which lingered on in her clothes, gave rise to quite different feelings, which were in perfect harmony with the landscape that surrounded them.

Snow covered the ground; the trees looked like ghosts in their winding-sheets; at intervals a starving wolf, alarmed by the tinkling of the sledge-bells, could be heard bounding away. In the steamy atmosphere of the carriage, Gaston and Kate, their lips glued to each other's, forgot – until the last staging post before Saski was announced – that the thermometer read thirty degrees of frost and that they had both left behind, one in Paris and the other in Warsaw, bonds which they were ever so slightly straining at that very moment.

The viscount had Kate put up in the finest lodgings the place could boast, embraced her tenderly, slipped into her handbag the price of a bunch of violets which she had refused to accept when they had set off and bade her wait patiently for the sledge that had brought them there and would take her back to Warsaw, when it had delivered him to Saski.

CHAPTER ELEVEN

When he crossed the threshold of Aunt Athene's drawing-room, Gaston fully expected a dressing down which his conscience told him he richly deserved. So he was very pleasantly surprised when his aunt held out her hand to him almost affectionately and said,

'The prodigal nephew returned at last! He must have remembered the old manor house and felt the need to relax a little and to breathe the air of our forests.'

'Above all, to see you again, dear Aunt; I have been deprived of that pleasure for far too long.'

'The doors of Saski have always been open to you, dear nephew.'

'And, as you see, I have come in through them.'

'Is this Paris of yours so wonderful, then, that you can't tear yourself away from it once you've got to know it?'

'Oh, yes. If you have once admired it, you won't want to leave it again, Aunt.'

'Really?'

'It's just as I say.'

'You have convinced me, Gaston, so much so that I am tempted to put it to the test and accompany you to Paris as soon as the travel bug next bites you.'

This was like a bolt from the blue to Gaston, who could not have been more nonplussed. He looked at

his Aunt, but she seemed perfectly serious and a somewhat out-of-place, if quite gracious, smile hovered
over her thin, pale lips.

'Fancy your having such ideas, Aunt. I am greatly
surprised but delighted at the prospect of showing
you round that beautiful city.'

'Talk to me about it, so I can prepare myself in
advance.'

Gaston talked to her for hours, describing the
enchantments of Paris. Her replies contained no
mention or even hint of Julia. He walked on air and
told himself that the bitter pill of the 150,000 francs
might slip down quite easily.

'I'll have to confess my sins to her,' he thought, but
there was no hurry and they went on chatting till
dinner-time.

It had been ordained that that day the viscount
should have one surprise after another. The fact that,
a few minutes before the majordomo threw open the
doors of the dining room, a ravishing young girl in
mourning and with the ease of manner of someone at
home in high society came into the drawing-room,
was by no means the least of these. She acknowledged
with a gracious nod of her head the introduction
which Aunt Athene made, as custom required, of her
nephew.

'Pani Wilhelmina de Sustabacka, the daughter of
one of my best friends, whom we had the misfortune
of losing a few months ago.'

The recollection of this sad event brought tears to
the eyes of the beautiful child, who had every right to
be called that as she was scarcely eighteen. Tall,
slender, graceful in her bearing, she was a creature of
exquisite distinction who impressed Gaston enormously, spoilt though he was by similar impressions
during his long stay in Paris. He did not wish to

appear inferior to this fine creature and spared no trouble to make himself as agreeable as possible. His aunt, too, was in good spirits. the dinner was delightful and Gaston had to admit that this young face very pleasantly lightened the atmosphere of the manor house and that her beautiful, bell-like voice warbled delightfully. So there was no talk of leaving and, after a fortnight, not a word of his confession had been uttered. All the same, eventually the matter became pressing and his aunt gave him an opening when she said to him one morning,

'My dear Gaston, I should like to know about the state of your finances. I have heard that life in Paris costs an arm and a leg. Yet you don't appear to have spent all that much.'

'That's because I have borrowed money.'

'A Saski in debt!'

'What would you have me do? Even a Saski who has no money needs to borrow.'

'Who are you in debt to?'

Gaston told the story of the 150,000 francs and spoke for a long time to explain the temptations of high life in Paris.

When his little speech was over, the aunt put on a solemn face and indicated that she would pay but on the strict understanding that he stayed with her till the spring, when she had decided to travel to France with him.

'So you are serious about that plan, Aunt?' he asked.

'Of course; didn't I say so?'

What was to be done? Gaston, at that moment, thought of Julia but he also thought of Don José's lawyer and it has to be confessed that he was in two minds about what to do.

We shall never know what his reply might have

been if he had not seen, through the pane in the door to the conservatory, the outline of Wilhelmina busy stripping a magnificent camellia of its dead leaves.

'I shall do just as you wish, Aunt,' he replied, bowing respectfully.

'In that case, give my man of business a list of your creditors; he will see to it that they are paid.'

'Just look, Aunt,' Gaston, who no longer heard a word of what the old spinster was saying, 'how beautiful your young friend is looking this morning.'

Athene glanced into the conservatory.

'Indeed,' she said, 'the poor child's beauty is a fatal gift of destiny.'

'Why do you say that?'

'Because the enormous fortune she was due to inherit on the death of her mother had been frittered away by foolish and frivolous deeds of sale she had signed, so that Wilhelmina is now as poor as a church mouse. I propose, when in Paris, to find her a position as a lady's companion and I count on you to help me in that. It would save her great financial embarrassment.'

'But, of course, Aunt, most willingly.'

From then on, Gaston regarded Wilhelmina as inevitably destined to tread the primrose path of the *demi-monde*, of those who have come down in the world.

The young woman went riding and naturally Gaston accompanied her; she showed herself to be very gracious but with that reserve customary in good society which did not allow certain subjects to be touched upon too directly. The result of these equestrian exercises was that Gaston's imagination became heated, that he was put on his mettle – in short, that he fell madly in love and wooed Wilhelmina with all the ardour of which he was capable. She responded to his transports – but platonically. She thought of marriage: Gaston, not in the slightest. What with his aunt's way of thinking, a penniless girl! Why, it was out of the question. It would be going from the frying pan into the fire. But making her his mistress was another matter entirely.

On this slippery slope, rapid progress was made, so much so that one day the young lady allowed herself to be given a kiss, then two and then three.

'Give me as many as you like,' she seemed to be saying. Gaston did not need to be told twice.

They used to hold their trysts in the ancestral hall. Hidden behind the tapestries, in the depths of the window recesses they spent delightful moments, so much so that one day Wilhelmina let herself drop on to the divan at the feet of Stanislas Saski, an imposing hero, whose portrait showed him as a warrior cased in steel, and . . . and . . . , sad to relate, the warrior's treacherous descendant plucked that flower of innocence, as only a short time before he had Mademoiselle Thorel's.

Only this time, by one of those accidents it is better not to look into too closely, Dame Athene appeared suddenly like the devil from a jack-in-the-box which so frightens children.

The viscount was no longer a baby but, all the same, the sight of the venerable old lady was truly disconcerting. He was still bent over the young woman, whose legs came down on either side of the divan and who was still swooning. There could be no doubt about the nature of the crime that old Stanislas Saski had just witnessed.

The young woman quickly stood up and, still bleeding, threw herself on her knees before her hostess, exclaiming,

'Forgive me, please forgive me. I did wrong but he promised to marry me.'

'What infamy! What sacrilege!' the aunt cried, pointing a minatory finger at the loving couple. 'This young girl entrusted to my care by her mother on her death-bed to be dishonoured by my nephew under my own roof! I must call curses down upon you.'

'Be merciful, please be merciful; he will make amends.'

'Gaston, you hear the child,' his aunt said severely. 'What do you say?'

'That I am at your feet in all obedience and that I shall do anything you see fit to order me to do to obtain your pardon.'

'There are no two ways about it: you must take the path of honour. You robbed this child of it, now you must restore it to her.'

Gaston inwardly cursed himself. Certainly Wilhelmina was charming but to marry a penniless girl in such circumstances and to lose Julia seemed extremely painful. But what could he say? What could he do?

'Aunt, this would be too much happiness for me,' he managed to stammer.

'Who knows whether it will bring you happiness or the opposite,' the old lady replied. 'In either case, you shall be the husband of Pani de Sustabacka within a fortnight or I shall banish you from my presence for ever.'

She had her way. A fortnight later the castle chapel, brilliantly lit, blessed the union of these two young people and there was no cloud on the bridegroom's brow because, when the marriage contract was signed, it turned out that the bride, far from being penniless, was one of the richest heiresses in Poland.

And Julia? Ah, Julia – this is what happened. The young woman felt her heart break, especially when she heard that the estate agent at Saski had settled the matter of the 150,000 francs with Don José's lawyer. She wept and the general consoled her as best he could.

Nevertheless, one morning, he found her the prey of black gloom mingled with fierce indignation.

'What's the matter, my child?' he asked.

'Read it for yourself, I haven't the strength to talk about it.'

The general read a letter from the same agent, sending Mademoiselle Thorel, on behalf of Viscount Saski, the sum of 150,000 francs in appreciation of the pleasant times spent together during his stay in Paris.

'I am sure the viscount had nothing to do with such an insult. Alas, I am afraid your happiness is in danger and you must prepare yourself for a rupture between you. But I am absolutely certain that this way of setting about it, which so rightly shocks you, is none of his doing. What do you propose to do?'

'Send it back with a note on the envelope saying "apparently sent to the wrong addressee" '.

'That's perfect, but send it to the viscount to make sure he gets to know about it.'

And so it was done.

To her surprise, Dame Athene one morning received the news that her attempt to dispense largesse had been unsuccessful. She thought that the amount had been considered inadequate and she raised it. This time, Julia did not even open the letter and the noble spinster was forced to acknowledge that if Mademoiselle Thoral was a foolish virgin, she certainly was not a venal one.

Her nephew's marriage was a *fait accompli* and he no longer feared he would escape the net. So she decided to hand over to him all the correspondence which she had held back. A lively altercation between nephew and aunt ensued – but what is done is done.

Gaston wrote an affectionate and repentant letter

to Julia, explaining what had happened, to which he received the following brief reply:

'No doubt it was ordained! Be happy.

JULIA'

Stung by the way the young woman took his absence, Gaston showed the letter to his aunt, who conceived a feeling of benevolent sympathy for the abandoned girl.

Some weeks passed. Julia had sold all the furniture of the rue de Courcelles house and moved into the apartment in the boulevard Saint-Michel, with the intention of living there on the proceeds of the sale, until a very advantageous share-holding in a bank, which Don José had promised to procure for her, should yield fruit.

This was the way things stood when the young woman had a message from Madame Briquart, who had not given her any sign of life since her departure from the rue d'Assas.

The message was: 'I have to speak to you. Come and see me.'

These few lines intrigued Viscountess Saniska greatly.

'What could she have to tell me?' she wondered. She soon found out.

Old Madame Briquart had received two visits: one from Pani Athene, which she did not mention to her niece, and the other from Don José, who came on official business to ask for the hand of her niece, Julia Thorel.

'But sir,' the good lady had stammered, somewhat bewildered, 'I don't know if I should . . .'

'Yes, madam, you should, because I know everything; and it is the dignified fashion in which Mademoiselle has just acted, linked with the qualities of heart and mind which I have learned to prize in her that have decided me to offer her the *fatherly support* (he stressed these words) of my aged arm. It will soon falter; but my death will assure her of a more than golden independence and, by giving her that, I shall have repaired the great injustice that fate has done her.'

'In that case, sir, I have nothing to do but thank Providence.'

'Ah, no, you can do another thing as well. You can help overcome your niece's scruples, if exaggerated delicacy on her part should give rise to them.'

'You may count on me.'

In the end, after a long discussion between aunt and niece, Julia agreed to become Dona José de Corriero.

'Undoubtedly some good genie has become mixed up in her affairs,' the colonel's lady said to herself after Julia's departure. 'But I think it is as well that I did not mention the little arrangement I have come to with Pani Saska; I could not, certainly, let Julia lose 200,000 francs, which she would obstinately have refused had she known about it. When I am no longer here, they will give her pleasure since she will assume they come from me.'

Athene was determined that the young woman, who had strayed from the paths of respectability on the strength of her nephew's promises, should not be subjected to an undignified existence, so she had devised this way of arranging everything, by making Madame Briquart the trustee of the money.

Thus ended the vicissitudes that attended the dawn of the adult lives of Madame Briquart's nieces, whose subsequent history we shall relate in the next volume.

VOLUME TWO

CHAPTER ONE

In the drawing-room of one of those houses half way
between a chateau and a villa of which there are
thousands around Paris, two young women seated at
a work-table were chatting, while adding a stitch or
two to one of those interminable tapestries which
seemed to share the fate of the *Revue des Deux-Mondes*
– never to be finished. One of them was a beautiful
brunette of about twenty-five with a matt complexion,
vivacious, deep-set eyes, gently waved black hair,
crimson and luscious lips revealing an ardent
temperament. The other, blonde as corn, did not look
as if her twentieth birthday was far behind her. She
had fine and delicate features, peaches-and-cream
cheeks, periwinkle-blue eyes and her smile was
imbued with one of those expressions full of childlike
candour which nevertheless, for no apparent reason,
arouses in the mind sentiments diametrically opposed
to those inspired by chastity. They were both wearing
elegant black dresses, which, though still of mourning,
were of the kind that did not wait for the ray of
sunshine of a good opportunity, to merge into purple
and then to yield place to pink. Both of them were
avidly inhaling the spring scents – streaming in
through the open window – of the Forest of Montmorency, on the edge of which the country house *Les
Charmettes* was situated.

'How beautiful spring is,' the younger one, Madame Florentine Vaudrez – the owner of the house in which they were – said.

'Yes,' replied her sister, Julia de Corriero, with poorly disguised off-handedness. She was presently staying at *Les Charmettes*.

'You don't seem to be convinced of what you are saying, my sister.'

'In truth, darling, I don't know what is the matter with me but for some time now – I don't know why – I have been very depressed.'

'Oh, my poor darling.'

'What would you have me say? I know it's madness but it is so. I am rich, accepted in a world I like; I have very good friends and all the same I am bored.'

'Perhaps it is still disappointment in love?'

'No, it's not what you think. From that point of view I am totally cured. I have completely forgotten the man who was not worthy of so great a love and of such complete devotion as mine. Only there is an immense void in my spirit and my heart. What about you, Florentine? You have been a widow for nearly two years and living like a recluse. Tell me frankly: when the wind brings us the balmy air it has been lavishing upon us for some days now, don't you feel a sudden tremor which seems to want to remind you that a woman is not made to live in such solitude, as we do, and not to vegetate – vegetate seems to be the right word – without the joys of love as we have been doing ever since those who taught us about the physical needs of mankind are no longer with us?'

'Oh yes,' Madame Vaudrez said in a tone of profound conviction, 'but all the same, I've got Baby.'

'Yes, during the day, but at night Baby is asleep. What about you, do you still do it?'

'No, certainly not, and you?'

'I often bite my sheets, my pillows and sometimes . . . my hand wanders and I force my imagination to help it along and make me forget about the real thing I miss. You are too innocent, my fair-haired little one to understand what I am trying to tell you.'

Florentine blushed to the roots of her hair and her smile which was full of confusion immediately made her sister ask a more precise question.

'Is it true, my love? . . . but really I ought to have remembered and to have guessed.'

'Remember what?'

'An exclamation that you allowed to escape you the day after your wedding, when poor Aunt Briquart told you were still a virgin though married since the day before. Don't you remember? . . . You said, "So it's possible to experience lively physical pleasures without a man taking part."'

'Oh, yes, it's coming back to me but where were you at the time?'

'In your dressing room, busy admiring your trousseau. But the cheval glass was turned towards the door and I could see the Colonel's lady set about clearing up all your doubts on these delicate matters.'

Florentine had gone crimson. Julia gave her a special look, half smiling, half blushing, drew her to herself with a caressing arm and said to her very softly, 'If we went up to your dressing room I could show you how the indiscreet mirror was placed.'

Florentine said nothing in reply but she got up and the two sisters went to the room in which Madame Vaudrez was initiated into the mysteries of love. This time, they no doubt decided that the cheval glass should not reflect what was going on in the bedroom, so they bolted the door between it and the dressing room.

'You are privileged,' Julia said in a slightly melan-

101

choly tone. 'The recollection of the sunny hours of your life is written on the walls of the house in which you live and where it looks as if you will end your days. Things are quite different with me. I have squandered my former happiness like so many rosary beads scattered over the highways of my life.'

'Isn't it engraved in your mind and is that not enough?'

'Perhaps you are right. In any case, it is not likely that our story has reached its final chapter.'

'Yours was delightful in its very first chapter. I have often envied you.'

'The joys and intoxications I experienced in the arms of Gaston Saski were ineffable, but what an awakening!'

'Forget all about anything that was not good, my darling,' Madame Vaudrez replied, in an effort to distract her sister's mind from the slippery slopes of introspection. 'Come here, close to me, and let me hug you like a baby, you big foolish thing.'

And suiting her action to her words, the young woman drew Madame de Corriero to the divan, made her sit down and smothered her eyes, mouth and ears with kisses. The mirror was opposite them.

'Look, Julia, how well your black hair goes with the golden silk of mine,' Florentine said.

'Indeed,' Julia answered and with a light hand removed the comb and pins that held up Florentine's hair while the latter loosened her sister's long tresses and let them cascade over her shoulders. These two silken waves mingled their contrasting colours and combined their balmy scents to produce the prettiest and the most voluptuous picture imaginable of these two charming and loving women.

'This little mark on your neck, my dear,' Florentine said as she undid the buttons of her sister's bodice, no doubt to see it better, 'I didn't know you had it. Oh, how pretty it is,' and the young woman kissed it.

'I think it greatly resembles the one you have just there on one of the charming rotundities which are crying out in vain to be unveiled.'

'I believe you are right: it should be easy to compare them.'

Julia with a nervous movement unhooked the black kid armour her sister was wearing. This operation resulted in exposing two firm, white breasts of irreproachable shape, the sight of which brought cries of admiration from Julia.

'Little sister,' she said. 'I have never looked upon you as a goddess of beauty but you are as fair as our mother Eve was said to have been. Let me admire you in the simple costume she was wearing, the day she made the conquest of the serpent.'

'Is there not going to be any reciprocity in these proceedings?'

'But of course, and we shall amuse ourselves by making *tableaux vivants* in front of the mirror with just one difference – the characters will wear a little less than those of Madame Rattizas.'

'We shall also have the advantage of being less exposed to weather conditions than the beauties who created flesh-and-blood sculptures in their garden.'

While talking like this, the young women had taken off all their garments; bodices and skirts were lying on the carpet side by side. Soon they were joined by corsets, stockings and shoes; then the cloud of cambric which was still in place, after a little hesitation, slid on to pink and white feet and uncovered in all their splendour two magnificent female bodies, each representing the ideal type of blonde and brunette beauty.

'How beautiful you are.'

'What a delicious creature!'

Such were the exclamations which escaped the lips of Madame Vaudrez and those of Madame Corriero.

For a moment the two women contemplated each other like two jousters sizing one another up. Then Julia seized her sister's waist, drew her to herself and started to kiss the nape of her neck in such a way as to excite the nervous centres. Then she continued with her gracious gesture as if making a necklace of her kisses for her until she eventually arrived at the breasts, the pert little heads of which were already standing up, avid for voluptuous pleasure.

'Oh, they are naughty,' she said, 'we shall have to chastise the wicked things.'

Julia took the two voluptuous objects between her lips one after the other and rolled them gently, producing sighs of beatitude from Florentine. After some moments employed like this, Florentine twisted out of the arms of her new kind of lover who pushed her as far as the divan and made her collapse on it.

'I bet that nobody has done to you what I am going to do now,' Julia said.

'What's that?'

'You'll find out and even see it. Look in the mirror.'

Florentine looked into the cheval glass and saw Julia, who, having deliberately excited her with her agile fingers, seized her thighs and falling on to her knees on the bearskin which surrounded her, covered the golden thicket of her love grotto with passionate kisses.

'Oh, what are you doing to me?'

'Not much . . . yet . . . but I want to make you die of happiness.'

And continuing this activity she passed an ardent tongue over the pink little hillock, which swelled under her caresses, and tickled it. She then moved her tongue with a steady to and fro movement so that after a little while it got as far as the entrance of the vagina.

Florentine no longer contented herself with giving out little sighs of satisfaction: she was now shouting out loud.

'Oh . . . my God . . . what is happening to me? . . . go on . . . I had no idea . . . go on . . . , more . . . faster . . . I never knew till now what delight and intoxication are . . . oh, my darling, don't stop.'

'Wait, you'll see, this is just the beginning,' said Julia who was only waiting for the psychological moment to strike her dramatic blow. She did not have long to wait. While caressing her sister she had stretched her out on the divan. When the swelling produced by the preliminary work made her decide it was opportune to bring about the final spasm, she got to work, and without stopping the movement of her tongue on the clitoris, she buried her finger deep in the crevice of love and by lively and quick movements brought to Florentine's lips the inarticulate but vibrant and prolonged moans, which lasted until the moment when her nervous strength ebbed completely.

Madame Vaudrez dropped her head on the cushion and did not even respond to her sister's embrace. Julia laughed and said to her,

'You are ready to sleep now, you selfish creature.'

But recriminations were in vain. Florentine did not move and Julia, still on her knees in front of her, was making every effort to revive her. Julia was greatly moved by the passion which she had just displayed and also by the concern she now felt for her sister, who looked so pale and prostrated. Suddenly she trembled and tried to stand up but two solid hands on her hips opposed her and she felt a loving tongue caressing her in her turn as she had caressed her sister.

'Oh, my God, who is that?'

'Let Madame keep still,' a familiar voice replied,

105

'It's me, Dorothy the maid. Oh, I have wanted to do this for a long time but didn't dare.'

'You seem to have made up your mind now,' Julia said. 'As you have begun so well, you might as well go on.'

She bent over Florentine's chest and thus even more conveniently offered up to the maid the two prominences with which nature had endowed her. Dorothy, who no longer needed to seduce her mistress, who was now perfectly pliant, artfully and without difficulty set about exciting her. Her tongue wandered about, went up and down, lost its way . . . nor did her fingers remain idle, either.

This activity could not continue for long without effect. Scarcely a few minutes had passed when Dorothy played her trump card. She quickly pulled up her skirts, displaying to Florentine who had somewhat recovered from her ecstasy and silently watched the strange scene taking place in front of her eyes, a magnificent masculine engine of perfect form and respectable proportions. She managed it like someone who had had considerable experience in using it and made it take the path of joy, an action which elicited from Julia a cry of voluptuous surprise, immediately followed by several others as Dorothy imparted to the instrument the natural motion of a vigorous male member.

'Ah, ah,' Julia cried out, perfectly matching the maid's movements. 'I am dying, I am melting with happiness, heavenly delights. Who is blessing me with his hot liquor of love? It's killing me; ah, ah!'

Dorothy, judging that her work had been done, now withdrew, let her skirts drop, then seized her mistress by the waist and laid her down on the divan beside her sister. A moment of silence supervened in the suite and all three profited by it to recover their equanimity, after which they looked at each other.

CHAPTER TWO

'May Madame forgive me if I have done wrong,'
Dorothy finally said respectfully but as if certain in
advance that she would be judged indulgently.
Dorothy was the faithful maid that Gaston Saski had
given Mademoiselle Thorel when the latter left her
cousin's house in order to go and live with him. Ever
since, Dorothy had looked after her mistress who
greatly appreciated her skills. She was one of those
people who had all the integrity of a certain type of
Parisian domestic servant. These are girls who know
all about the intimate affairs of their employers but
still manage to preserve the air of well-trained,
discreet servants. They combine with it the tolerance
of close confidantes who – in return for a comfortable
life in accordance with their station and the courtesy
on the part of those they serve – will not betray their
masters' or mistresses' weaknesses any more than they
would impose on them an embarrassing degree of
familiarity.

'Oh, Dorothy, tell me how it is that you are here,'
Madame de Corriero asked. 'I thought you were doing
the shopping in Paris and in any case I had bolted
Madame Vaudrez's bedroom.'

'I had finished my shopping and I came in by the
unlocked door of the servants' staircase.'

'I had always thought that butter wouldn't melt in your mouth – how wrong one can be!'

Dorothy smiled. 'That sometimes happens to the cleverest of us. It all happened by accident. As usual, I came in without making a noise and naturally I looked at what was going on in front of me. What I saw was so pretty that I did not have the heart to retire discreetly. I looked at the marvellous things that were happening and regaling my eyes; as I have a great deal of experience in such matters, I foresaw right from the start that Madame Vaudrez would not repay Madame in the same coin, and so I decided to take her place.'

'Oh,' Julia said, 'and how did you manage to do what you did? I felt something – I don't know what – but it certainly suggested nothing feminine.'

'It would be easy to show the ladies my *modus operandi*, if they so wish,' Dorothy answered.

'But of course, certainly,' the two sisters, who were very intrigued, replied enthusiastically.

Thus encouraged, Dorothy obliged and without abandoning her respectful bearing, lifted her skirts up to her hips and displayed a body stocking which, in contrast to what English women wear, held more than it promised and was equipped with a solidly-buckled leather belt with two straps passing between the thighs. Its function was to support a fine set of male genitalia made of rubber, flexible and sturdy at one and the same time.

'Well, isn't that curious,' the two women said.

'But,' objected Julia, whose recollection of the experience she had just undergone still puzzled her, 'I did feel a hot sensation which such an inert instrument would not be able to produce.'

'Madame is mistaken, the two globes representing the reservoirs where the liquor of love is produced in men are filled with luke-warm milk or syrup. When I press them with my hand, a liquid intended to complete the illusion spurts out.'

'Dorothy, you are quite forgiven,' Julia said.

'Madame is very good and can rely on my discretion; but please allow me to tell the ladies that those who are young, beautiful, rich and free should not spend their time using artificial aids which may ruin their health. To be content with illusion when one can so easily enjoy reality itself – that is something I cannot understand.'

'Steady on, Dorothy, how you do go on. Don't you know that getting married again is a very serious matter?'

'Getting married again! Good Lord, who said anything about that! No, no – no ties, just a lover you change if he ceases to please, but to whom you abandon your body and soul when he seduces you.'

'What if the world should find out about these comings and goings of love? What would it say?'

'It would forgive a permanent liaison which is regarded as a sort of marriage. If you should be in luck and the first one works out, well and good. But if not, what does it matter?'

'But if, instead of the admirable person you thought you had met and with whom you had hoped to live in perfect physical and moral harmony, you discovered in the cold light of the following morning that the man in whose arms you had spent the night was not such as to give you the joys that you were seeking, you would have compromised yourself and lost the esteem of the people around you. All that for the sake of changing a lover.'

'It is easy to avoid disagreements.'

'Dorothy, if you know how to achieve that, I implore you to tell me at once, because I assure you that I infinitely prefer the passionate caresses of a man to all the subterfuges which imagination makes us resort to as a substitute.'

'As for me,' Florentine interrupted, still in a state of ecstasy, 'I have never had such supreme delight as just now even in the arms of Cherub.'

'What do you mean, Cherub?' Julia asked in astonishment.

'Never mind,' Florentine said, annoyed with herself at having said so much.

'But he's only three years old.'

'I'm not talking about him but about his father.'

'About his father! What, poor George? Is it him that you call Cherub?' Julia started to laugh, so much so that her sister was in the end forced to say:

'Oh no, it is of Gaétan d'Hérissez that I am speaking.'

'I don't believe it.'

Julia said to herself as she recalled her adventure at Saint-Jean-de-Luz, 'I have actually always thought it extraordinary that George should have sired my beautiful nephew.'

'Well, well,' she said aloud, 'and I never knew anything about it. Where did you get to know him?'

'At Saint-Gildas, but I'll tell you all about that. All you need to know is that the day when . . . ,well, when it happened . . . Gaétan was still entitled to an orange blossom wreath.'

'How sweet; now I understand why you gave your son the gentle nickname of Cherub.'

'And I,' Dorothy said to herself, 'now know why he looks so much like the Duke.'

'So, Dorothy,' Julia returned to their original topic of conversation, 'you say you have found a way by which we can give ourselves up to the delights of a

110

love affair without our adventures becoming a scandal in our little circle.'

'Oh, there will be a lot of scandal, but as nobody will know that you are its heroines, you will be all the more amused.'

'I must confess I am completely mystified.'

'I shall explain myself more clearly.'

Dorothy spoke for a long time and with much good sense. She made it clear to the ladies how with their money and her own discreet devotion it would be possible to transform an old house that Julia owned in the Ile Saint Louis in the Marais into a house of enchantment. She had inspected it all, from the courtyard to the loft, on the day that Madame had sent her to take back the keys from the last tenant who had the courage to stay in the sad rue Charles V. She was familiar with the entrances and exits and she knew that the staircases of the basement debouched on to a deserted alleyway, which made the mysteries of the comings and goings difficult to penetrate, and, moreover the garden lent itself to a thousand combinations.

'I can assure Madame,' she concluded, 'that nothing would be easier to organise. To put any snoopers off the scent, we could register the house as being rented to Madame Félicité Deschamps, my real name, which nobody has heard for at least twenty years. Believe me, ladies, this is a far better thing than to destroy your health, which will certainly come about, if what happened just now were to be frequently repeated.'

'Bah, what difference could that make?'

'An enormous one as far as the nervous system is concerned. This is not an old wives' tale I am telling you. I have qualified as a midwife and was one of the star pupils in the obstetrics school.'

'So why on earth are you a domestic servant?'

'Because I was mad and impetuous and so lost my job.'

'Tell us about it, Dorothy.'

'If it would amuse the ladies, I am quite ready to do and it won't take long. I had a lover of whom I was very fond, one of the housemen in the school. There was another whom I loved very much less, but who loved me a great deal and whom I had an interest in keeping sweet. He was one of my teachers. One evening I went to Bullier's with Marcel, the houseman. While I was dancing he got terribly tipsy and wouldn't take me home. I left him to sleep it off and went home alone, forgetting that he had a duplicate key to my little flat. I had not taken more than a few steps when I found myself face to face with Paulus, my professor — "Where are you going?" — "I'm going back home." — "How unwise to go out dancing all by yourself, a young girl like you." — He lectured me and came back to my place to spend the night.

'We went to bed, spoke sweet nothings to each other and finally went to sleep. But towards morning I heard a light sound at the door and then steps in my room. It was Marcel who was ashamed of his behaviour the night before and had come to make his excuses. Seeing that I did not move, he undressed without a sound, slipped into bed and relaxed. I was between the devil and the deep blue sea. The situation, funny though it may seem in retrospect, was extremely awkward. Marcel, who was still the worse for drink, fell fast asleep. Paulus, tired by our amorous exertions, was sleeping soundly, too, but I was wide awake. Any moment, they would both turn on me and Paulus in particular — he had a violent temper — would get his own back on me at a particularly unfortunate time, because it was on the eve of the exams. What was I to do? I decided to escape.

'Very quietly I got out of bed, got dressed and decamped. Nobody punished me but at daybreak Marcel, still quite sleepy and naturally believing me to be beside him, wanted to make it up with me and stretched out a daring hand towards my hidden charms,' Dorothy said with extremely comic gravity. 'Paulus at first believed that this was a caress from me and lent himself to it with good grace. He was about to reciprocate the gesture when an oath rang out and the two men sat up in bed and exchanged the most salty insults. I heard about this afterwards from my neighbour. And here were my two lovers furious with each other and accusing each other of sodomy. The matter did not come to court. Explanations were made but the scandal in the Latin Quarter was so great that I was thrown out of the Midwifery School.

'This is the reason, ladies, why I today have the honour of serving you instead of having a good consulting room, horses, a house and rents coming in like a good many of my fellow-students.'

'Oh well, Dorothy,' Julia said, 'don't lose hope of still having some of all that because I promise you if you make your idea for the rue Charles V work well, I shall not prove to be ungenerous. Do you agree, Florentine?'

'Yes, of course. I am very keen on trying it out together with you but you know, my darling sister, only on condition that from time to time . . . we do what we did just then.'

'Agreed.'

Dorothy proceeded to dress her mistress and Madame Vaudrez. An hour later, no one would have suspected on seeing these two women in the drawing room, so perfectly distinguished in their bearing, that he was looking at two people who – just an hour before – had been maddened by unbridled lust.

CHAPTER THREE

Two months later in one of the small rooms of the Cercle de Paris, Messrs de Lyncent, de Melreuse, de Laigle, de Restorff and Maxence de Berny, a very elegant staff captain, the darling and spoilt child of the ladies of the Paris *demi-monde* and even of Paris society, were foregathered. All these cheerful men of the world sat in more or less congenial groups with a smile on, and a cigar between, their lips, listening to a tale told them by a good-looking fair man called Raoul de Paliseul, who was sitting at a table covered with newspapers.

'That Raoul,' de Melreuse muttered, 'always has the most amazing adventures. What an imagination that boy has.'

'You don't believe me, gentlemen. Well, I assure you everything I said is gospel truth,' the young man insisted. A hint of stupidity could be detected in his speech.

'At the time of post-chaises and highway robberies before 1830 this sort of thing might have happened, but as for our day – get away with you! Raoul, you are trying to fool us, my good fellow. All the same as your story is amusing enough, do go on,' Lyncent said.

'Well, if you're going to interrupt me from the very

115

start of this purely factual account – and I insist that's what it is – I prefer not to.'

'Go on, don't upset yourself. As it is a factual account, we shall keep mum, we promise,' everybody exclaimed. 'We shall send the first man who speaks to Coventry, even if Raoul tells us one of the adventures of Baron Münchhausen and presents it as sober fact.'

'Paliseul, dear Paliseul, go on with your story, do! You told us that three days ago, when you woke up, you found in your letterbox a letter written on English paper, impeccably and correctly composed, monogrammed with a gold sphinx and scented with a rare, unfamiliar and very expensive-smelling perfume. That the letter asked you – if your courage and your discretion were up to it – to go on foot to the avenue MacMahon at about two o'clock in the afternoon, where you were to speak to a lady who would show you a card decorated with a sphinx and scented like the letter.'

'Melreuse, you have missed your vocation. You will never become a Marshal of France, but you would have made a first class stenographer.'

'What can I do? Sometimes parents are mistaken about the aptitudes of their children. But the ball is now in your court, so continue with your little story.'

'At a canter, gentlemen. And it was at a canter that I took myself off to this mysterious rendezvous, in spite of the instructions I had been given to use a slower method of locomotion – going on foot. Only, as one must not needlessly antagonise people, particularly in the matter of details . . .'

'The only things that anyone attaches any importance to,' interrupted Lyncent.

'Order, order! No interruptions! Silence, gentlemen, silence!'

Paliseul went on when calm was restored.

'As I wanted to show just how capable I was of meticulously obeying instructions, I made my carriage stop at the rue de Tilsit and from there I went on foot to the avenue bearing the name of the brave Marshal. I had hardly been there for ten minutes, wondering what was going to happen, what marvellous proposition some society lady might make to me, or what young virgin, tired of being one, an Ephesian matron was going to put at my disposal . . .

'In the midst of these wise but sad thoughts, a ray of hope appeared. The style of the letter, the attractiveness of the paper, its scent, seemed to presage something less banal than I was familiar with. I was busy with my reflections when the course of my reverie was interrupted by the arrival of a magnificent and elegant carriage which appeared to have been made in London. This smart vehicle came up at a quick trot, drawn by two superb horses, driven by a coachman as black as ebony, wearing a black livery, trimmed with old gold and on the buttons of which, as on the doors of the vehicle and on the letter I had received that morning, there was a golden sphinx. The coupé stopped abruptly about twenty steps from where I was. My heart was beating a little faster, I swear to you. Who was going to get off this vehicle? I wondered.'

'Yes, yes, Paliseul, we appreciate your intimate thoughts at that moment, but do get on with your story.'

'I intend to, but no trimming has ever spoilt good material.'

'If we keep interrupting, he will never get to the end of his story,' Monsieur de Restorff threw in.

'A lady alighted,' Paliseul resumed.

117

'Ah, there she is now, with her feet on the ground,' Melreuse murmured.

'Yes, I saw a person of indeterminate age, heavily-veiled and dressed like a wealthy middle-class woman, from which you could tell nothing very much, advance towards me. If this was to be my heroine, I had been cheated and I'd make a getaway, I told myself. This impression grew stronger, but it then vanished when I noted that the person who was about to address me, belonged to the same nationality as the blackamoor whose face had a vague resemblance to the sphinx, on the unknown woman's writing paper. The black lady looked at me attentively, then with a deliberate step walked straight up to me and handed me a card which was exactly as described in the letter.

' "Monsieur de Paliseul?" she asked, evidently for form's sake, because the witch knew perfectly well who I was.

' "Himself, Madame," I replied to that very unseductive person, putting an enormous block of ice between her and me by my studious courtesy.

' "Would your lordship be kind enough to smell the scent by which he will recognise me." She handed me a calling card of a design identical with that described in the letter.

' "That's quite unnecessary: I shall take your word for it and I hope you will promptly explain to me what this mystery means. It seems to me we are taking on the air of conspirators. Have you at least brought a white wig and a black collar? I find these things missing for a role which, I must warn you, is completely new to me."

' "These little props will not be needed. The wings of love will suffice to disguise us."

'She said "us". A tremor of horror seized hold of my entire being.

118

' "So be it," I answered. "If it is under the banner of him who conquers us all that we must fight, I shall enlist very willingly but, dear Madame, as I am not good at playing guessing games I should be much obliged to you if you were to tell me something about it."

' "With pleasure. I am here to do just that – my mission to you is that of a go-between."

' "That is what I suspected."

'All the same, I breathed more freely after this avowal and my attitude lost some of its mistrust, but deep down I returned to my first doubts and secretly wondered who the society lady in financial difficulties, and honouring me with her kindness, might be.

' "My mistress," the negress said, "is a foreigner."

' "Which means she is not from this country."

' "As your lordship, who I see is in a playful mood, says."

'So she understood. I became suspicious of this blackamoor. "On what heights of Montmartre or Belleville has this one learnt the subtleties of the French language?" I asked myself.

' "Madame," she continued "belongs to the high aristocracy of her nation and cannot, because of her position, form any intimate relationships in her circle – if I may so express myself."

' "Please do, your information is full of mystery in one sense but, taken as a whole, is limpidly clear."

' "So Monsieur understands me."

' "Perfectly. You were saying that Madame . . . ?"

' "Madame Granada."

' "The devil, it is a name that burns like the Andalusian sun. It is evident that the one who bears it cannot be fond of intimate – as you put it so delicately – deprivation, Madame . . . ?"

' "Félicité, at your service, your lordship."

' "Madame Félicité, is your mistress pretty, young and intelligent? There is no point in asking you whether she is a brunette or a blonde. What with the pseudonym she has given herself, she must have the eyes of a *Madrilène* and raven-coloured hair." '

"'That, in fact, is what she looks like but at the same time she is one of the most beautiful women in Paris and she is twenty-five." '

' "Ah, the season of delicious fruit, Madame Félicité." '

' "She has to go to a great deal of trouble to reconcile the conventions of society with her personal satisfactions." '

' "All the same, this charming person is taking great risks, you must admit, because if I were not what I am, a gallant gentleman, all sorts of disaster might occur." '

' "Oh sir, Madame knows full well who she is dealing with." '

' "Indeed? So this beautiful foreigner knows me?" '

' "Very well." '

' "Stuff and nonsense!" '

' "She has done, for two years." '

'I would not believe her but Madame Félicité supplied me with a wealth of details about my private life which left no room for doubt. I was known, very well known indeed.

' "In that case," I replied, "there is nothing for me to do but express my appreciation to Madame Granada and to thank her for the benevolence with which her beautiful eyes have condescended to look upon me." '

' "But there is one more thing." '

' "What's that?" '

' "To give your word as a gentleman that you will never try and find out who she is." '

' "Discretion is my middle name and I undertake to do as you ask. I promise that even if by any chance I should in future find myself in the presence of the beautiful Granada, I will give no sign of recognition unless she expressly authorises me to do so."

' "Oh, that is not enough. You must undertake never to try and lift the mask which will constantly cover her features."

' "Your mistress, good lady, seems not to be in her right mind. She wants to remain veiled in front of what you call an intimate friend?"

' "Yes, as far as her face is concerned."

' "Ah, her face only."

' "Yes."

' "And the rest?"

' "From time to time she will disrobe."

' "I admit that in that case there may be some compensation." '

'What a devil that Paliseul is,' Melrouse murmured.

'Shameless and even dishonest,' de Laigle commented.

'Keep quiet, you chatterboxes,' Lyncent grumbled. 'Carry on, Paliseul, with your very instructive story.'

' "So," ' Paliseul went on, ' "Madame Granada, you believe, will receive me unclothed?"

' "When our Mother Eve heard the words of the serpent in the Garden of Eden was she dressed by Worth?"

' "No, no, what you are saying is very sensible and I give you all the promises you demand. I agree to everything and I am burning with desire to go to the goddess who feels herself to be sufficiently beautiful to dare present herself in this original fashion."

' "In that case, there is nothing more for me to do than to pass on to your lordship the invitation extended by my mistress to come and take a dish of tea with her. This evening I shall be at the same place at 9 o'clock and I shall lead you to her."

'I had a previous engagement that night but as the adventure had begun to intrigue me, I decided to accept the invitation. I promised to be there and the black maid left, leaving me wondering how it was all going to end.

'No financial considerations were mentioned in all that went on. As she knew me, whoever it was must have been aware that, apart from flowers and chocolates which were *de rigueur* in such cases, I could afford nothing else. Was this woman purely and simply an eccentric, or did they want to draw me into some trap? I decided that the latter was at least possible and that I would take a revolver with me in any case.'

'Oh love, thou hast lost me Troy,' an unknown voice whispered, 'but in the nineteenth century thou art scarcely going to cost anyone his head.'

'At nine o'clock precisely,' Paliseul went on, without taking any notice of the interruption, 'I was at the avenue MacMahon, and some minutes later in the sphinx-emblazoned *coupé* sitting next to the negress, whom I more and more suspected of not being what she seemed. I was scarcely seated when she lowered all the blinds so that I could not make out where I was being taken. We did any number of detours and travelled for at least half an hour when I heard a whistle. I gave a start.

' "Don't be afraid," my guide told me. "The coachman is dumb and this is his method of asking the doorkeeper to let him in. We have arrived." And in fact I heard a heavy gate move on its hinges, the vehicle was swallowed up in some vaulted structure and stopped at the bottom of a huge white marble staircase. Its wrought-iron banisters reached to the very top and had a very grand air. A large number of flowers in enormous vases of old Rouen ware cheered up the scene, and large lanterns of the same style as the banisters, lit up the staircase.

'But I have been speaking for a long time, gentlemen, I fear I may be tiring you.'

'You have chosen absolutely the right moment to stop, as in a cliff-hanger serial in the *Figaro*, Paliseul. All the same, we demand that you continue.'

'All right then, I shall take a breather for a moment before obeying your command.'

'A glass of syrup and water for the speaker who is delicately hinting at how inconsiderate of him we have been.'

CHAPTER FOUR

'The dwelling I had just entered was nothing like the common run of modern buildings, as I told you, *messieurs*,' Monsieur de Paliseul went on. 'It seemed very grand. It had to be in a very quiet quarter because no sound could be heard from the outside. In this house there was a silence which might have seemed cold but for the profusion of lights and of plants which cheered it up.

' "Would his lordship care to go up?" I was asked. I followed Madame Félicité through an antechamber, which was austerely decorated, and then into a small waiting-room hung with oriental fabrics. At last . . .'

'Yes, at last, what happened?'

'At last, the door opened and my guide announced Viscount Paliseul. I found myself in an annexe which must certainly have belonged to the palace of the Thousand and One Nights, facing a woman, half lying on a chaise-longue and dressed in the most delightful negligé of white velvet and cerise satin, which only a dressmaker maddened with love could have dreamed up.

'A mask covered her face but her arms emerged naked from wide sleeves lined with red, and what arms they were! They must have been the ones the Venus de Milo had lost. A firm and abundant bosom brimmed over a bodice scarcely fastened by three ribbon bows. In her hair there were a few flowers. Altogether, she presented a perfect picture of voluptuousness, but with nothing to suggest the vulgarity of a whore. I was in a large and high-ceilinged room entirely covered with reseda velvet on which whimsical arabesques of flowers in lively colours — opulent red petals above delightfully coloured leaves — were climbing up. From the ceiling in the shape of an awning, rich hangings dropped down and were lost in the shadows of the corners of the room. A thousand charming bibelots and the most comfortable furniture were grouped in its nooks and corners.

' "Welcome to the home of a recluse," she said to me in her melodious voice, as she stretched out to me a small aristocratic hand decorated only with a wedding ring.

' "A recluse you may be, but your hermitage does not seem very austere to me," I said with my most seductive smile. "I cannot be too grateful for the honour you have accorded me in allowing me to share it with you for a while."

' "Who knows, this may not be your opinion in a few days' time."

'I looked at her with keen attention: she was an admirably beautiful woman with a magnificent figure and all of her indicated the habits of a woman from the highest circles. I waved away her suggestion with a dismissive gesture.

' "Sit down here," my charming hostess said to me, "we shall chat a bit before taking tea."

'I was now ensconced quite close to the mysterious woman, who seemed to feel quite at her ease in spite of the odd circumstances that had brought us together. By the time black Félicité appeared to announce that tea was being served, we had become bosom friends. She talked away merrily and although

125

Madame was a foreigner, she turned out to be extremely well-informed about all the gossip of Paris society. Some of the time she seemed to me to be using Teutonic consonants, but as I am not much of a linguist I could not make up my mind whether they were genuine or not.

'The beautiful Granada got up. I offered her my arm which started to tremble and we went to a little dining room, very small, in the middle of which was an elegant table with a fine supper laid on it. The room gave on to a bedroom beyond a curtained doorway. There I could see a large ebony bed raised on a red velvet-covered dais and half drowned in the mysterious rays of an Algerian lamp. It was quite clear to me that I could dispense with preliminary courtesies, let myself go without fear of disgracing myself and give way to the stirrings in my loins which I began to feel quite unmistakeably.

' "Viscount," the lovely girl said to me when we were at table and eating crayfish and *paté de foie gras*, a tea that seemed more like supper, "we shall banish all ceremony. What is your name?"

' "Raoul, my dear Granada."

' "Well then, my dear Raoul, what would you say to a short stay in my domain?"

' "I think I would regard myself as the happiest of mortals and already the intoxication of happiness has overpowered me to the point where I am losing my head."

'To prove this I reinforced my speech with two tender kisses planted on her beautiful breasts, the contours of which I could see. The young woman made a movement which was so gentle that it was clear to me I could afford to be bold. A few moments later we were eating from the same plate and drinking from the same glass. Sitting on my knees, Granada

126

seemed to be only slightly worried about the comings and going of my hands and as the pink bows of her bodice were in my way, I undid them, and saw a tiny belt of red satin edged with snow-white lace which held up the breastplate of a shift of diaphanous cambric. A single buckle held this miniature corset and I undid the hook. Oh my God, my whole being trembles at the memory. I slid my hand round the supple and curvaceous waist, the nerves of which I felt tensing with intense passion.

' "Granada, my adored one," I murmured, "I am seeing you for the first time but already I love you."

'Granada smiled and put her arms around my neck.

' "Ah, your fiery lips, I want to devour them," and my lips were clasped on to hers and I became drunk with the balmy breath that escaped her chest.

' "Your breasts, darling, what a marvel. I respect this horrible mask because I promised I would, but don't forget what I was told: the rest . . . "

' "Belongs to you," she murmured in a deliciously emotional voice.

' "You must be splendidly beautiful," I said, but as I belonged to the circle of the disciples of St Thomas I wanted to see in order to believe.

'The negligé of white fluffy stuff treacherously deserted the shoulders it had been charged to protect and left me absolutely staggered by the sight of the most beautiful female bosom that I had ever been called upon to adore.

'Her breasts could rival those of Diomedes's slave and the avid little nipples stood up. I felt little shivers run over her skin and my kisses which soon became mad and delirious added to the effect.

'A simple button on each shoulder held up the shift, a feeble defence which gave way in no time.

'The garment and the linen – everything slid on to

127

the carpet. In my arms there remained a magnificent figure trembling with desire and voluptuousness.

' "Granada," I said, pointing to the bed which seemed to be offering itself to us and was bathed in that gently filtered light which is so propitious to amorous dallying, "would you like to . . . ?"

' "Yes," my charming hostess murmured.

'I picked her up in my arms and without ceasing to caress her I carried her into that beckoning room. Then I put her down on the great ebony bed, where I very quickly also freed myself from the shackles civilisation imposes upon us and intermingled my legs with hers.

'I voluptuously drank at her delightful breasts in great gulps; I swallowed the intoxicating juices of the petals of her love grotto and with a sensation of delight hitherto unknown to me I felt a young, ardent, impetuous creature, giving free rein to the feelings which moved her, vibrate in my arms.'

'Who is Granada?'

'Perhaps I shall never know. However, what I do know is that this woman is one of those frank natures that do not just allow themselves to be taken but know how to give themselves. My friends, I left this mysterious house with my soul ravished, my senses maddened and I will be the unhappiest of men if I never see her again.'

'What do you mean,' the listeners exclaimed in chorus, ' " – if you don't see her again?" Did this strange Granada just want a one-night stand?'

'I don't know because when we parted and I besought her to tell me when I would see her again, she said, "When the sphinx writes to you," and now I am waiting.'

'A day or two of rest will do you good, my dear Raoul. You have rings under your eyes which your love adventures have stamped on your face in a positively indecent fashion.'

Throughout Raoul de Paliseul's account, Maxence de Berny had said nothing and contented himself with looking at Raoul in a very strange way.

When he fell silent, Maxence approached and held out his hand to him.

'My compliments, Raoul,' he said. 'You have a rare talent as a storyteller, much verve and elegance of diction, an enchanting voice and a marvellous imagination, but in spite of all that, you are never going to convince us, because the story you tell is not true. You are just spinning yarns and, on top of that, you're bragging.'

'How dare you say that?'

'Only because it is so. I also know the beautiful anonymous one, the sphinx and the mysterious house. I spent the night before yesterday there and I know that you were not there.'

'What you say goes beyond the bounds of reason.'

'Say what you like, but the facts are as they are, and I shall prove it.'

The audience became breathless. It had been a long time since the circle had had such an entertaining evening.

'Well, go on, prove it then,' Raoul said, somewhat vexed and disturbed.

'First of all,' Melreuse said 'let us establish the basic facts of the matter. What day was it that Raoul was supposed to have been made happy?'

'The sixth.'

'And Maxence?'

'The sixth.'

'You both had tea?'

'Yes,' the two of them replied with a laugh.

'Well, let Maxence take the floor.'

'As far as the introduction is concerned, my story is identical with Raoul's. I too had a mysterious letter with a sphinx seal, a black carriage, an identical maid and a calling card with a sphinx on it. Just a moment, here it is.'

'And here's mine,' Raoul said feverishly.

'My children,' Melreuse intervened in a conciliatory tone, 'you were both called and both chosen, that's all.'

'But surely not at the same hour.'

'Yes, that does seem a bit strange.'

'After that,' Maxence resumed 'Raoul gave us exciting details but they were devoid of truth. The beautiful unknown was not called Granada at all but Pervenche or Periwinkle. She was not born in the shadow of the fiery spires of ancient Iberia, but under the sky that produces the Northern lights. It was the most delicious moonlight imaginable when she took off – I do not know how many yards of cambric which made up her clothing – that Eve emerging from the snows of the Jungfrau, an Eve naive and curious at the same time, in whom the surprise of ingenuousness was mingled with all the skill of a courtesan. There was nothing impetuous about her but with so much delightful wheedling and coaxing, so much womanliness in the woman . . .'

'They're both quite mad about their Dulcinea,' De Laigle and De Restorff said to each other.

'Maxence, the matter is an enigma wrapped in mystery and as the Circle of Artichokes cannot tolerate mysteries we must clear it up. On the one hand, we have Raoul who claims to have been in the seventh heaven in the company of a brunette. Maxence, in equal detail, maintains that at the very same moment, at the same place, he had the same experience with a blonde. My children, does not all this suggest the handiwork of a competent pimp?'

'No, no,' the two young men said at the same time, 'it's nothing like that.'

'Even the servants refused tips and I,' Raoul said, 'next morning received back by post the cheque – for an appreciable sum – which I had deposited on the mantleshelf, thinking that I was acting discreetly.'

'Well, then it remains a mystery, my friends.'

'Yes, a mystery which intrigues me enormously,' Raoul said.

'Me, too,' Maxence said, adding, 'and I promise you to leave no stone unturned to plumb it. The day after tomorrow I shall keep a sharp look out and I shall tell you what I find out.'

'What is this?' Paliseul said in an anxious tone of voice, 'you are supposed to go there the day after tomorrow?'

'Yes.'

'You had a letter from the sphinx this morning then?'

'No, we arranged a meeting before we parted.'

'That was a good thing to have done; I wish I had. You were wiser than I.'

'But you have hope.'

'Yes, I have and I shall cling to it while waiting for better things. Is your rendezvous in the Avenue MacMahon?'

'No, this time I have to go . . . but hold on. Let us be discreet and circumspect and let me not repay the benevolence with which the charming Periwinkle honours me, with indiscretion . . . Since she wants to maintain her anonymity, it would be improper to put jokers like you on the track of her secrets.'

These words produced a wave of indignation.

'What about the solidarity of the Circle?'

131

'I'm not much concerned about that. Moreover, the Gospel says "seek and ye shall find". Put this divine recommendation into practice, gentlemen, and whatever you discover will be your rightful prize. As for me, I shall leave you free to prepare your plan of campaign.'

Whereupon Maxence shook hands with his friends and left the little drawing-room reserved for the use of the Artichokes.

After his departure Paliseul remained pensive for a moment.

'This Maxence,' he said resentfully,' has the luck of the devil. What has he got, I ask you, to be such a favourite with the women?'

'Why, Paliseul,' Melreuse objected, 'it seems to me that you have nothing to envy him for.'

'Perhaps not, but in my case it never lasts long,' he murmured in reply. 'One or two trysts – when it is not a question of paying for my pleasures – and then I am dismissed. With him it is quite different.'

'What can you do, women are flighty creatures – if the old adage is to be believed. I'll recite a little verse to you.'

'Don't bother; I know it:

    "Woman ever for variety lusts,
    He must be mad who in her trusts." '

'So, my good friend, if you haven't the satisfaction of inspiring lasting passions, at least you are spared the trouble of having to extricate yourself from unwanted ties.'

'Well, gentlemen, we shall see what we shall see, but I promise you that I shall be less cagey than Maxence.'

CHAPTER FIVE

It was not only in the Circle of Artichokes that confidences were being exchanged. In the little boudoir of a pretty apartment in the Boulevard St-Michel the two women who so intrigued these gentlemen were also talking and the murmur of their conversation mingled with the bursts of laughter which it produced.

'Why, Julia,' Florentine said to her, 'didn't you come to *Les Charmettes* to tell me your impressions of the day before yesterday?'

'I was completely taken aback when I came out of our mysterious retreat, by that gloomy cellar staircase that Dorothy makes us use, at not finding you in the carriage.'

'I told Dorothy to warn you I wouldn't be there. Could she have forgotten to tell you?'

'No, your maid never forgets anything. She told me that you were tired but I didn't believe her. What was the matter with you?'

'Oh nothing very definite, but I had a mass of calls to make that I couldn't get out of, and also I wanted to think.'

'Think about what?'

'This enterprise, so full of dangers, which is intended to overcome the vexations of widowhood by permanent fantasies. What about you? Were you disappointed with the evening you spent?'

'Yes, I think I was. I confess I did not recover the intoxication that I experienced in the arms of Gaston in those of Raoul de Paliseul. There was some temporary sensual satisfaction but once that had passed I felt I had taken the wrong step. What can I say? I don't want to see that great blond, insipid fellow again. He's all façade. His solid frame conceals nothing worthwhile. Is it because my physical shape and his don't match, I wonder? In any case, I don't want to discuss it any more. Yesterday I waltzed with him twice at Madame de Bourmond's; during all that time I looked at him, saying to myself, 'If only he knew.'

'At least he didn't recognise you, did he?'

'No, our precautions worked well. But you, my love, what have you to say about your evening?'

'Oh, I was enchanted with Maxence. He is charming, obliging, delicate and in his arms I tasted all the happiness that one can hope for from love . . . from a man . . . Provided that . . .'

'Ah, yes that Cherub should remain your only child. Is that it?'

'Well, yes, that delicate point is a worry.'

'Nonsense, nothing venture – nothing gain. In the last resort, if the worst should come to the worst, you could always make a long journey and everything would be all right. Will you be seeing Maxence again?'

'Tomorrow, and I look forward to it enormously because I think he knows how to love me as I need to be loved.'

'And how is that?'

'Lots of caresses rather than . . .'

'You unfortunate child, your tastes are absolutely deplorable. These charming preliminaries to which you refer produce the same effect as the consumption of aperitifs unaccompanied by a substantial meal'.

'Not if you know how to set about it'.

'Oh what sophistication – it quite amuses me. Is it Dorothy who taught you it?'

'No. On the contrary, she maintains that I will kill myself or will age before my time if I continue to prefer the enjoyments resulting from amorous refinement to natural ones . . . but this does not stop me being capable of loving a man truly, if he understands what I want.'

'Whatever you do, don't reveal our secret.'

'Don't worry about that.'

'You see, with your head on the pillow, it is difficult to have secrets from your beloved.'

'All the same, I shall continue having them, however well-beloved he may become. And whom are you going to summon to the feast, since the unfortunate Paliseul is in disgrace?'

'I don't know yet. That's what I am thinking about.'

'I will leave you to your meditation and will join Cherub in the Luxembourg Gardens.'

The two sisters parted and Julia gave orders for the carriage to be got ready to take her to the *Salon des Beaux Arts* where there was an exhibition which had only opened a few days before. If there was a show which drew the crowds this surely was it. It was not only artists and amateurs who flocked there, which was natural, but during the first few days the rooms were invaded by a crowd of people whose enthusiasm was difficult to understand when you heard all the nonsense that they were saying to each other in their little groups.

This torrent of idle strollers occasionally dried up, and the gallery, at certain hours, once again became the meeting place of elegant society which went there on the way to or from the Bois de Boulogne, in order to take a rest and to cheer itself up by the sight of beautiful things – while refreshing itself with a glass of Malaga and some pastries.

Madame de Corriero was no artist in the absolute sense of the word: she did not know how to handle a brush and she had never manipulated a chisel but she had, to a supreme degree, an aesthetic sense as well as a very highly-developed sense of poetry. She truly appreciated certain works, especially those in which the author, who is strong enough to seize hold of an arresting thought, encapsulates it in a form that will mirror it for all eternity.

Instinctively she felt drawn to those artists whose works were dredged up from the depths of their soul and were not inspired merely by cold intelligence and learning.

The young woman, having offered a small sacrifice to the god of gluttony, began to wander from room to room distractedly looking to the left and right. Here she would pout contemptuously, and there she would stop, captivated by something and looking at it for a long time. For several moments she stayed immobile in front of a picture of quite large proportions which undoubtedly the jury had not appreciated because it was badly placed. All the same it was a charming canvas. It was no great thing: just the corner of a wood, a lilac bush and two young lovers, one of whom seemed very anxious to convince the other of the intensity of his sentiments. There was nothing special or classical in the treatment; it was a simple impression of a morning, the light of a beautiful rising sun playing in the foliage, rousing the clusters of lilacs and lightly brushing with its warm caress the face of the lover, a splendid-looking young man.

Julia, completely charmed, opened her catalogue to see who this work was by, as on an impulse she felt tempted to buy it. But suddenly she stopped what she was doing and looked nonplussed, because she saw before her in the flesh, and smiling, the young man in the picture, who greeted her half-respectfully, half-teasingly and said to her:

'Madame, since this picture seems to interest you, allow me to spare you the trouble of enquiring about the identity of the artist. He is Michel Lompret – at your service if you think him worthy of it.'

Michel Lompret, on becoming a man, had fulfilled the promise of his adolescence. He was no longer the king of creation in springtime but personified summer in all its splendour. Tall, slender, with broad shoulders, nervous fine hands and small feet, he perfectly typified the qualities of elegance and strength. His striking features were framed by abundant black hair and a magnificent fair beard, very well cared for and elegantly divided in two in the Russian fashion, allowing his fleshy great lips, which seemed to be inviting kisses, to be seen.

The young man's blue eyes remained fixed on Madame de Corriero and showed an admiration which was perhaps a little too intense for irreproachable propriety but was absolutely frank. Women are instantly disposed to be indulgent when they notice that they have made such an impression on anybody.

'Sir,' Madame de Corriero said in a reserved tone of voice but with no trace of annoyance in it, 'I thank you very sincerely for your courteous offer; however, I should not wish to take up your time in spite of the curiosity which the striking resemblance between you and one of the figures in the picture arouses in me.'

'How happy you make me by saying that. So you think I resemble this young man? What you say has rejuvenated me by a good ten years.'

'What, so this is not a matter of pure chance?'

137

'No, that is myself at twenty, with a little country neighbour who inspired my first love at sixteen,' he added with a smile which contained a shade of melancholy.

'What, is it you who painted this?'

'Yes, I have that honour or misfortune, whichever you consider appropriate.'

'Good fortune is the right word and this picture, which is redolent of spring and fresh morning scents, marks the dawn of your talent, Monsieur Lompret. You have not yet passed through the last stage of your career in art but, as I am in a strange mood and we have become acquainted in a way which is outside all the rules of etiquette, I shall confess to you that I am curious to know how the romance, the first chapter of which you seemed to be relating so eloquently in the shade of these delightful lilac bushes, ended.'

Michel hesitated for a moment, then he smiled. 'Can we ever drop anchor in the ocean of time for even one day?'

'So time, in its dreary fashion, accomplished its work of destruction in this case, too?'

'Not as you suppose, I think, but "she lived like a rose, just the space of a morning". It was on the anniversary of our first kiss that I conceived the idea of painting this picture which I hoped would be more successful. Look where they have hung it.'

'Did that prevent me from noticing it?'

'You are right: I am wrong to complain.'

'The jury's decision to hang it in such an obscure position will not stop me from acquiring it, if you agree.'

'To sell it, even to so charming a lady, is out of the question, but I should be only too happy if you would accept it as a gift.'

'That,' Julia snapped, 'is not a matter that concerns

you: it is with the gallery that I propose to negotiate. As for you, Monsieur Michel, I am charmed to have made your acquaintance and I shall order things in such a way that you will not regret having met me.'

So saying, Madame de Corriero made a gesture which announced her intention of ending the conversation.

'Oh but yes, I will regret it, if I am not to see you again.'

'See me again! What a strange idea!'

'I see nothing strange in it. I am an artist and not a gentleman. You are lovely as no other. As for me, where I see a vision of the ideal, I lose my head as far as social conventions, but – believe me – not respect, are concerned, because it is a sense of worship I feel which threatens to invade my heart and my head.'

'Really,' Julia said with a smile, 'so whenever you love, you respect?'

'But of course, because I adore when I love.'

'Have a care; you have just told me that you are going to adore me.'

'How do I know what I am saying? I think that you are going to go away and that perhaps I shall never see you again and that breaks my heart.'

'Oh, but this is serious, it seems . . . and since you assure me that you will always respect me I have a fancy to . . .'

'To do what, please tell me?'

'To call upon you to explain to me your theories of love; they seem to me to have the merit of being original.'

'Oh, how good it would be of you to do that . . . but . . . here . . . it would be difficult, I need a little time to discuss the matter and the gallery is about to close.'

'That is true, oh well . . . but are you a discreet fellow? The world is a wicked place and perhaps you do not understand all the demands it makes.'

'Madame, I am the son of General Lompret,' the young man replied with considerable dignity.

'In that case, the last of my scruples is removed. Promise me, sir, not to make me repent of my whim to hear what you have to say, to which I am yielding by allowing you to wait for me at the exit of the gallery.'

Michel saluted her with the most worldly courtesy and left. Some minutes later he saw Madame de Corriero arrive and glance around her to assure herself that she could see no familiar face. She made a sign to him to approach and surprised him by inviting him into the pretty crested coupé which was waiting a little distance from the exit.

In a low voice the young woman gave orders to the groom and Michel, surprised but charmed by the turn that the adventure was taking, felt himself being taken at a fast trot by a superb team of horses, the rapid strides of which quickly got them beyond the fortifications of Paris.

'Sir,' Julia said when the sound of the vehicle going over the cobblestones had stopped, 'you know that I am expecting from you a course on your theories of love. I am listening.'

'Ah, Madame, you appear to be so intelligent. How can you speak to me like that? these are burning issues which cannot be discussed with a cool head; they are matters of the religion of the heart, the only true religion, the adoration of beauty and the madness of love.'

'A somewhat pagan religion, you must admit.'

'Paganism must have had something to be said for it, as the other religions which followed it were sufficiently inspired by it to show us that a complete creature is very different from a eunuch.'

'You appear to be fervent in all things.'

'Yes, I love what makes my heart beat faster. The artist, you see, is a creature apart; in his brain, there seethes a world of sensations peculiar to himself, born out of almost complete indifference to external objects. We are all a little like Victor Hugo's dreamer; like him the artist can cry:

> *'Yes I am the dreamer, I am the comrade*
> *Of the little golden flowers, of the crumbling wall.*
> *I speak to the trees and the wind; they all know me*
> *In May when the scents of the bowers are wafted abroad.*
> *It is then I have my chats with the stock flowers,*
> *It is then I get advice from the ivy and the cornflower.'*

'And what do these pretty advisers tell you?'

'That everything which is not in direct communion with nature is bad because the vibrations deriving from the great loving harmony of that same nature are the only ones blessed by Him who has created all. They tell me that we are guilty when we resist the impression made by these vibrations. There is a strange correlation between those which strike the brain of the artist and those which reach his heart. How quickly his imagination takes flight! It is amazing how it carries him away as the result of some vision seen like a glimpse of his ideal – a vision which almost always, alas, is followed by disillusion, because sooner or later the veil is torn and the adored creature is transformed into a vulgar little simpleton who had never understood the sensual expression of the visionary's sentiments.

'The poor madman, he had like Sully Proudhomme's poet hung a lyre string on to what he saw.

Like him he said, "Let us listen: everything is breathing." Alas, no, it was only his own voice and it was for this reason that very few of us are called upon to taste the delights of love in sacred plenitude.

'We often feel its physical sensations and sometimes a brief poetic illusion of love but, as for real love, that divine flame which gushes forth from the brain to invade the entire spiritual and physical being and which produces a state of intoxication so profound it makes one want to die, that is a delirium practically unknown to us, who understand it so well, because our sensations are produced, developed and exercised in a social circle which rarely responds to them with understanding.'

Michel felt what he was saying so deeply that he perfectly illustrated Boileau's aphorism:

That which one sees clearly is clearly expressed
And the words to do so come without effort.

His clear and elegant speech, his vibrant accents, his looks animated by an inner fire began to electrify the atmosphere.

'Do you know that you are on the point of convincing me?' Madame de Corriero said half laughing and half seriously. 'And that you will leave me persuaded that you are one of that small number who really know how to love?'

'In all things I try to put into practice my evangelic precepts, and I do to others as I would be done by.'

'One can't in good conscience ask for more. And now, allow me to ask you if in your life, which I suspect has been adventurous, you have heard the echo of your being, or should I say the echo of your soul?'

'You are right, because if behind my forehead there

lurks an invisible and present soul, it is through my senses that I extend it so that it can be perceived,' he said with a laugh. 'To answer your question, no, I have sought, I have knocked at doors, but I have not yet found the pure gold that I have always desired, that I have always pursued but which disappeared like a mirage in the Sahara, at the very moment I was about to seize it. I am beginning to fear that I shall die before I capture it.'

'Never despair. This is wise advice which I take the liberty of giving you.'

'Minerva could not have spoken better, but do you understand what I am trying to say when I tell you that I must respect before I can adore.'

'I believe so.'

'Oh. I am sure of it. Your face cannot deceive. You are not an ordinary woman and you know well that when one loves one is mad, one is intoxicated by the beloved, one devours her with one's caresses, one seizes her as one surrenders to her. The contemplation of her beauty makes one idolatrous; everything that voluptuousness teaches love is heaped upon her and one enjoys it in her arms.'

This manner of speaking was new to Julia. Michel was the first artist who had confided his intimate thoughts to her. She had never heard from the lips of a votary of art this cry of love which requires a certain superiority of mind to be uttered, and which is so delicious that the ears of those who have been caressed by it are unlikely to hear anything like it elsewhere.

She was moved, more than the situation called for. So while he was speaking, she could not take her eyes off a lock of hair fluttering on the neck of the young man, who had taken her hand in his. She did not withdraw. He kissed it and she did not object. She thought, 'What for?' Michel, had he heard the question, would have answered, 'If the spring could say why it murmured, if the morning could say what made it happy and if the evening breezes could tell their secret, then perhaps we should know what women really think when they pretend they are thinking of nothing.'

Truth obliges us to say that Julia simply thought that it would give her enormous pleasure to kiss that little intriguing lock which time and again tickled her neighbour's ear.

Meanwhile time was getting on and the carriage was going towards some destination that Michel did not bother his head about.

Suddenly it stopped. Julia jotted down a few words on a card, slid it into one of those minute envelopes which foresighted women always carry with them and after having passed the note to the servant who awaited her orders respectfully, she said to him, 'For Madame and at once.'

The carriage and the servants diappeared. Michel and Madame de Corriero were at the edge of a wood, part of an ancient forest but one in which the sap still rises abundantly.

'Where are we, if I may ask without indiscretion?' Michel said.

'At the far end of the Forest of Bondy,' Julia replied with a laugh. 'Are you scared, by any chance?'

'Of myself perhaps; but you must know that there is no one braver than a fool once he has got going, so have no worries on that score.'

'You can see that we are under thick foliage which ought to appeal to your artistic soul.'

'Not very much. I am not the man for great forests; they crush me with their mysterious majesty. I find in them a mixture of ugliness and of beauty which shocks me. The appeal of these giants is not for me.

I love the sun, the light, the open air, beautiful shapes. All that poetry of wood nymphs and dryads, all that vegetation with a thick bark, leaves me cold. I enjoy much more wandering among tall grass, among corn and supple stalks which when they press against us seem to caress us.

'Having in my arms a woman I love, both of us touched by the gentle powers, each one of which tells us: love, love, *that* is the great law of the Universe! That I think is heaven.

'But am I not boring you with all my reveries? It is you who wanted me to importune you, so you must not be vexed that I have tried to plumb your soul before telling you that you are the most beautiful among the beautiful, which is how I should certainly have begun my conversation with any other woman.'

'That is not what I want – far from it. You are opening up my mind to unknown horizons and you have revealed to me love, in a form as seductive as it is novel to me.'

'You are too charming not to have been loved and not to have loved.'

'I shall be frank enough to say I have, but nothing similar to the vision which you evoke has made my heart beat and I regret that, because I believe, in fact, that only those who love in that way, have found the secret of happiness.'

'If you would allow me.'

'What?'

'To initiate you into the intense delights, the roots of which are nourished by the springs of the mind.'

'So be it. We have known each other for only a few hours and yet I feel like your confidante and friend, as if we had known each other for a long time.'

'Much better than that, because we are on solid ground with each other – that of natural affinity.'

145

'Well, in that case, you won't find it unseemly if as a matter of course I take you to dine with me.'

Michel blushed.

'Certainly not, but where?'

'At my place, anywhere else would be out of the question,' Madame de Corriero replied with a certain degree of haughtiness.

'Well, let us do so today, but will you in your turn come and see me in my studio?'

'With pleasure.'

'That is very good of you, my dear comrade. Now will you tell me what I must call you when the grand word 'Madame' seems too formal to me?'

'Call me Sauvageonne – the wild one,' she said.

'Sauvageonne is a soubriquet which is hardly fitting, because it seems to me that you belong to the civilised world.'

'Not all that much; as you can see, before I got to know you I could not distinguish gaslight from sunlight.'

'Let it be Sauvageonne then.'

'Well said, friend Michel. Give me your arm and let us quickly go towards the path that you see below.'

'On our way,' the young man gaily answered, more and more enchanted with his adventure.

Soon they were in a broad avenue of elms which led to an old Louis XIII chateau, which successive owners had subjected to such transformations that it was now more like a villa than an imposing castle. However that may be, it looked charming.

The setting sun turned its large windows red, making them look like incandescent furnaces and drowning the roof in its rays. The avenue meandered through one of those parks which, though less dramatic than the virgin forest of the New World, are nevertheless not manicured like the baskets of a

Parisian florist and where weeds and ivy had corners reserved for them in which they could freely disport themselves.

As in almost all the important edifices of that period, a great basin, which the gardener pompously called the lake, stretched in front of the house.

Aquatic birds played on the edges, which were everywhere abundantly decorated with flowers and reeds, the leaves of which partly covered an old greenish Neptune, which had been going mouldy for a long time in the water and to which the birds paid scant respect.

'What a pretty place!' Michel exclaimed. 'You are lucky to live here.'

'It is not mine,' Julia answered. 'It belongs to one of my relations who is at present away and who lent it to me.'

They were at *Les Charmettes*, it is perhaps unnecessary to explain.

The carriage which had brought Julia had previously taken Florentine to the Boulevard St-Michel and, acting on the orders they had received, the domestic staff served Madame de Corriero as if she had been the mistress of the house.

A few moments were spent in the drawing room; then, after having given his opinion about the pictures which were there, and having done justice to the dinner like a well brought-up and witty man, Michel found himself *à deux* with Sauvageonne – to his indescribable pleasure. He started to ask himself, 'How is all this going to end?' He almost feared that too rapid developments in their relationship might destroy the impression he had got in contact with this woman, young, beautiful, well brought-up, so elegant and whom fate had made cross his path.

But nothing of the sort happened.

The conversation became very friendly again and hand in hand they leafed through the book of the heart that had first been opened during their journey there; they measured each other with their looks, they made music, dissected the poets, laying bare the hearts of some and dismissing others and when eleven o'clock struck and the footman opened the door to announce that the carriage was at Monsieur Lompret's disposal, Michel rose.

'Dear Madame,' he said, 'I do not want to know who you are: what does a name matter? You are what I see and I shall not ask your servants any questions, you may be sure of that, but I take with me Sauvageonne's promise that the day after tomorrow she will take a bachelor's luncheon with me in my studio and I thank her with all my heart for the gracious reception she has just accorded me. We shall meet again soon, shan't we?'

'I only have my word to give and I have given it. We'll meet the day after tomorrow.'

Michel left in a transport of joy and Julia returned to the suite she was occupying at *Les Charmettes*, no longer with that sense of moral void of which she had lately complained but entirely engrossed in the possible consequences of the day's happenings.

CHAPTER SIX

While Julia was flirting with Michel Lompret in the field of art, Florentine devoted herself to Maxence and had set the scene for him in her own fashion.

The following day when the young man arrived in the rue Charles V, instead of introducing him directly to the pretty Pompadour bedroom, Dorothy let him into the small boudoir which was furnished in such a way, so as to hint delicately at what one dared not say outright, namely that love has any number of ways of expressing itself, of providing voluptuous delights . . . and that . . . and that . . . the lady Periwinkle infinitely preferred those which the depravity of the senses, or rather the imagination has invented, to the simple proceedings inspired by nature.

She had told herself logically enough, 'What I am doing here has no other object but my personal satisfaction. Why then should I accept caresses which are less agreeable to me than those of my dreams. I might as well get married again and not run the risks of an unforeseen and compromising incident. If Maxence does not lend himself to my fantasies, well, then, then he will not hear from the sphinx again – that's all, and I shall look for another to share my pleasures.

Julia must be pursuing some new adventure. I can't wait till tomorrow to find out what she had in mind when she asked me to leave *Les Charmettes*.'

149

During the young woman's soliloquy as related above, Dorothy, the black carriage and the black coachman were at work and in accordance with instructions received the faithful maid let Maxence de Berny kick his heels in a room of the apartment which was unfamiliar to him. It was a sort of small drawing-room in octagonal sections and covered in matt silk of a dark granite colour. In the corners were strands of golden ivy, and a divan of the same shade followed the contours of the walls in oriental fasion.

A charming Dresden china chandelier shed a frank light on the pictures and statuettes which made up the ornamentation of this room, in the middle of which an enormous brazier was burning. Its fuel was mixed with aromatic herbs filling the atmosphere with heady scents.

'Madame asks his lordship to wait,' Dorothy said before withdrawing.

Maxence resigned himself to this and looked all round him.

'This is a room which proclaims the artist from a mile away,' he said to himself. 'This is a good starting point, because women like this are rare in Paris. A perfectly brought-up blonde. Come now, it's going to be child's play to plumb this mystery and to find out who she is.

'The devil! It seems to me, that the subjects chosen are not at all suitable for girls' boarding schools. What is that statue which all by itself constitutes the decoration of an entire panel? It is Venus making advances to poor Mars in the company of the beautiful Aglaea. This marble statue is so good it seems alive. It looks as if the goddess enjoyed lasciviously contemplating the charms of the Queen of Graces. Oh, and down there, what is that picture – or rather that draft? For, though the painting shows a skilful hand it is still only in sketch form, and here in the corner there is something which has nothing in common with classical art. It is some beauty giving herself up to the sweet pastime of solitary pleasure. She is offering up a sacrifice, while being the burnt offering at the same time. It is not kind of you, young lady, to keep to yourself so many good things a young man would be delighted to share with you. To judge from the ecstasy on the face of the young woman the artist must have caught her at precisely the right moment. Lucky fellow!

'Decidedly this collection in Madame Periwinkle's boudoir is all of a kind; here again we have a daughter of Eve who seems to have forgotten the precepts of Moses and not to fear the punishments with which the lecherous eating forbidden fruit are threatened; only this one has an accomplice, so there is at least some progress towards sound principles. She is ravishing, this great beautiful woman lying on an animal skin divan and the two legs with which she has made a necklace for him are perfectly rounded. Come, my good fellow, a little bit of vigour with your tongue, what the hell. I know that the exercise which you are engaged in will put you into a violent state of excitement, but let us hope that it will not end up too cruelly frustrating for you.

'The painter has admirably caught the expression of bliss in the woman's face. The man leaves something to be desired, which is understandable. The ideal type of masculine beauty has not yet been discovered and there is a gap to be bridged between the powerful form of Hercules and the effeminate attractions of the Apollo of Belvedere.

'How I am being made to hang about! Still it's nice to think that Madame Periwinkle is waiting for me.'

Maxence went on examining the miniatures; then

he passed on to the albums and found them filled with the most seductive images, all of which however, showed a tendency towards the practices of lesbianism. This fact plunged him into deep reflection.

'What can it mean?' he asked himself, 'and what is the purpose of this session I am made to undergo, among all these votaries of the cult of Lesbos?'

Suddenly, like a flash of lightning, a thought crossed his mind. He had come across an album filled with amorous scenes in which a couple deliver themselves up to all possible carnal pleasures, with the exception only of the one, that holds out the hope of life in the womb as a result of love-making.

'This is certainly the last word on earthly pleasures, the alpha and omega of love.'

All was quite clear to him now.

'I am being given a lesson, I can see that, and I am entirely ready to profit by it . . . Madame Periwinkle, your way of looking at things is in no way opposed to my sentiments. I shall do every single thing that is demanded of me but all the same do not forget that reciprocity in all these things is essential. If that is the way things are, we shall soon see whether I am an adept pupil, capable of putting into effect these indirect lessons.

'I was very clumsy the day I first adored the goddess who is mistress of this house but, what the devil, I had no idea who I was dealing with. If she had been a woman just starting out on a life of pleasure, I might have seemed depraved and had she been a priestess of Venus posing as a *grande dame* – not respectful enough. It was all very delicate. But now I know. Those blue eyes, so pure and so candid, are the false mirror of a soul which isn't candid at all.'

Dorothy now came to relieve the Count of his vigil and interrupted his monologue.

'Would Milord be good enough to follow me,' she said.

Maxence was introduced into the boudoir of maroon velvet, upholstered and draped with pink satin in which he had been received a few days previously.

Periwinkle, idly stretched out on a *chaise-longue* seemed determined to justify her nickname. She was dressed in a negligé of Indian muslin as delicately-coloured as the flower from which she took her name. The ample and flowing folds of light and diaphanous material showed the fine cambric night-dress and the waves of lace which, at the same time as decorating it, seemed to have broken out of their veiled retreat in order to prance upon the garment and to frolic with the butterflies of ribbons which surrounded it.

A nosegay of periwinkles emerged from the bodice, and her hair was strewn with them.

As far as the mask, with which her face was covered, allowed it – her features, her neck, her arms, her peach-coloured hands – emerged deliciously from their pretty frame, and harmonised perfectly with her fair flesh tints.

The picture conjured up a vision of freshness as in the corner of a wood covered with little stars of purple dog-tooth, when the sun lights them up with its luminous rays.

'Oh, how wicked you are,' Maxence said after having for a long time kissed the pretty lips offered him. 'To have made me wait so long is unpardonable, given that for three days I have thought of nothing but of the moment when I would see my little Periwinkle again.'

'Pooh, did you really give me that much thought? Admit that all your preoccupation with me did not stop you assiduously paying court to Mademoiselle de Versenges yesterday, and that the day before at the opera you had a mysterious assignation in a stage box, at the very back of which some lady, no doubt a great beauty, was carefully concealed.'

'How do you know all that? But first of all I swear to you that nothing disrespectful to you took place.'

'My dear Maxence, you must not think that I am in the slightest bit jealous. I am only anxious that your male stupidity should not be allowed the satisfaction of supposing that I shall take as gospel truth the fine phrases with which men are so free.'

'So we were together at Dr Vareil's and at the opera. How could I have failed to guess?'

'Don't you know that love is blind?'

'Tell me seriously, were you there?'

'I did not say that.'

'All the same . . .'

'All the same, I note that your passion has not yet reached its paroxysm because it does not make you instinctively more lucid.'

'I am lucid enough to know that you are the prettiest periwinkle I have ever seen. But you are the wicked one, you who look as if butter wouldn't melt in your mouth. What a sense of design you have. Your dress, my lovely, is a masterpiece of simplicity and your bedroom is a marvel of coquettishness. These hangings on an ivory base on which nosegays of roses and periwinkles dance like butterflies, this ceiling with draperies coming down from it in the form of a tent, and the fantastic old Dresden china chandelier dancing a mad saraband in the middle of it all, are enough to drive one wild.'

'I see that you remember the places through which you have passed.'

'There are not many details that escape me.'

'Really?'

'Yes, and if you wish we shall see together how good my memory is.'

'So be it, I shall be very glad to test you.'

Periwinkle got up from her *chaise longue* and embraced by the caressing hands of Maxence followed him into the bedroom.

'Look,' the young man said, 'there is a huge cheval glass here which certainly wasn't there when I had the good fortune to penetrate into the sanctuary of beauty last time.'

'But it was.'

'Little Periwinkle, you are telling me fibs.'

'No, I assure you, it is just that Félicité had forgotten to put in its correct place.'

'Ah, so this is its correct place, just opposite the bed.'

'Yes,' Florentine answered, blushing slightly.

'Well, that's different then. Is it at least a good mirror? Does it truly reflect what goes on around it?'

'You'll be able to judge that.'

'Just a moment, my love.'

While talking, Maxence moved a foraging hand among the lace and the ribbons of the negligé and established that the shift was only fixed by a few bows, which he quickly mastered. The looking glass proved that it was a good one, reflecting amid a cloud of lilac, the lilies and roses of the charming body of the young woman, as well as the golden and crinkly tufts of the silky fleece framing the sweetest little cavern of love that a maddened voluptuary could have dreamed of.

Maxence had decided to prove that he was not ignorant in matters of love and he started by covering the breasts of the young woman with kisses. He rolled the little red berries, which stood up in their midst like raspberries in a bowl of cream, between his fiery lips, and then his hands wandered . . . With his fingers

155

he combed the silky tufts of the young woman's armpits.

Florentine allowed it all to happen with good grace and her eyes, fixed on the looking glass, missed none of Maxence's movements.

The latter had placed her on the bed. Soon he seized her, put her across the bed and on her back. Florentine responded to his movements and, with the small of her back raised by a pillow and with her eyes fixed on the top of the large mirror, she drowned herself in the sensation of bliss of which she was beginning to feel the first signs.

Maxence, on his knees on a wolf-skin rug, busied himself separating the silken tufts among which his caressing finger was wandering and, when he had parted them, he applied his mouth to the little hillock of love which was stiffening as a result of the cunning suction he applied to it, rolling it gently between his lips as he had done with her nipples.

The young woman let out a cry of satisfaction. 'Ah,' she said, 'that is good, go on.'

'I was not wrong,' Maxence thought, 'I was intended to pass through the fields of Lesbos.' As he soliloquised thus, he continued with his gentle efforts.

'Ah, how good this is,' Periwinkle exclaimed from time to time ecstatically. 'Not too fast, I want this to last for ever. Oh, oh, my darling, your tongue, I can feel it, I want your teeth as well, nibble me.'

And Maxence obeyed, lovingly pressing between his lips the most deliciously-scented peach he had ever tasted. It was young and fresh like a delicious fruit gathered direct from the tree on a June day.

Motherhood had scarcely affected the young woman and it could clearly be seen that no sexual brutality had dulled the sensibility of her delicate organs.

156

Soon Maxence concentrated his efforts on the clitoris, the only seat of pleasure for a young girl but one which, in a mature woman, shares its sensual delights with its neighbour, the vagina.

His tongue from time to time plunged into the hot and rich depths of the canal leading to the womb, until the voluptuous spasm changed its nature and combined with that produced by the finger gently stroking the clitoris.

Florentine was in her seventh heaven. What she was experiencing under these knowledgeable caresses surpassed in intensity what she had felt under Julia's ministrations.

'Oh, how delicious this is!' she exclaimed, 'if you go on like this, I won't be able to hold back, you know, I shan't have the strength . . . it will be impossible for me, Maxence . . . my darling . . .'

In spite of all the satisfaction which the young woman felt at the experience she was undergoing, she wanted to raise herself up but two gentle, yet strong hands pushed her back; in any case, the crisis of pleasure was beginning. Maxence could feel the organs of love contract under his lips.

'Ah!', Periwinkle suddenly exclaimed, 'I am coming . . . I am dying . . .'

Accelerating the movement of his tongue, the young man now brought his moustache into play, which so far had been a mere witness and not an accomplice. Periwinkle twisted, while at the same time groaning with pleasure and flooding her lover with the hot effluvium which seemed to stream from her entire body to concentrate in her vagina. Enveloping everything for a last time in an enormous suck, Maxence was presented with the very soul of this gentle woman, who swooned with the greatest grace possible, without bothering about the state in which her companion might be.

The latter cut a sorry figure because a sense of delicacy prevented him from appeasing his sensual and strongly over-excited appetites.

'Since she prefers the artificial to the natural even when she is animated by passion, she would find such a proceeding all the more distasteful in the cold light of day, but I can't possibly ask her to reciprocate.'

His discomfort did not last long. As if Florentine in that ecstatic slumber had read his mind, she sat up and, passing her hands round the young man's back, she embraced him passionately.

'Oh my beloved, how I adore you. How happy you have made me.'

And her mouth drank in Maxence's breath. She took off the last few garments the young man had kept on. She rubbed her little nose in the rough fleece covering Maxence's body and finally her caresses took on the nature that Monsieur de Berny desired.

Soon Florentine slid down to the bottom of the bed, pushed him back and made him fall on to the divan placed near them. There she returned the caresses she had just received. She kissed him and bit him gently, wetting his apples of love with fragrant saliva and, in spite of her inexperience, she put the young man into a state of delirium close to pain.

A feeling of shame, understandable in the circumstances, stopped him from abandoning himself completely to the voluptous feeling that she aroused.

'Come now, my love,' Florentine finally said, 'I thirst for you, I want to taste the life-giving fluid which I have been told is so delicious. Pour it into me.' And the curious young woman worked so hard and so effectively that once more the devil was able to say: 'What a woman wants, God wants, too.'

The assault had been lively and the combatants were somewhat out of breath. So it was with genuine satisfaction that the two champions sat down in front of the little table covered with refreshing titbits to which they both did justice. After which Maxence looked intently at Periwinkle and Periwinkle looked at Maxence.

'Did you know, my lovely one, that you are the most deceptive still water that a man is likely to come across?'

'And why is that?' the young woman asked naively.

'Why? Because, my little mask, you have just with the delicacy of a little girl trained by the serpent, made me cross the Rubicon of my fantasies of voluptuous refinement – and all that in just a moment. It almost makes me feel guilty.'

'Really, I do not understand you.'

'But you do. Still, if in the end you have nothing to regret, then I need feel nothing but pleasure.'

'In that case you can imitate the example of David when he wanted to honour the ark of the covenant, because I regret absolutely nothing. I believe that whoever can do the greater, must needs do the lesser to make the greater possible, and should do it whenever he can.'

'I was sure of it, you little devil. So it is never to be any different?'

'I won't say never because I don't want to be selfish, but I will say rarely, because the method we employed today strikes me as being attractive and less dangerous in its consequences.'

'Indeed,' Maxence said with a laugh. 'By this system we shall have no heirs and, dear child, if – as I think – you have reason to be careful I will undertake on my honour', Maxence was now speaking seriously, 'never to make you regret the favours with

159

which you honour me. I will not conceal from you that I feel myself drawn to you by profound sympathy which our actual dealings with each other has done nothing but to increase. I profess the same amorous doctrines as you. Also, far from being shocked by your precocious tastes, which I discovered today, I was enchanted by them. The only thing that bothers me is this: will I never enjoy your trust sufficiently to see you drop your mask which hides your features from me?'

'No, Maxence, don't ask me to do that; if you do, we shall not be able to meet again.'

'I won't insist, but I assure you that I find this mask bothersome.'

'But not too much, I hope.'

'Thy will be done, little despot. All the same I hope that when we know each other better you will become more merciful. But tell me, who made the voluptuous pictures in your boudoir?'

'I don't know. I expressed a wish to have pictures of this kind to Félicité and she got them for me.'

'Félicité, the Moorish lady?'

'Yes.'

'I should like to have some like them.'

'She will readily agree to buy you some.'

'Ah, I know you suspect that through the painter I might get a clue to the mystery with which you surround yourself. But I shall solve the puzzle sooner or later, you may be sure. I warn you that the Circle of Artichokes is intrigued by the mysterious rendezvous given to two of its members, of which your servant is one, by a sphinx worthy of her name – and when those lads have got the bit between their teeth, they won't let go so easily.'

'Two rendezvous? I assure you, Maxence, that it was not I who . . .'

'Oh, I am sure of it, because the other beauty is as dark as you are fair; also she is called Granada, that daughter of Andalusia, a pseudonym that hardly fits you. But, little blonde, you must know who I'm talking about. Poor Paliseul is desperate, he has had no word from the sphinx and has lost his appetite.'

'Certainly, I have seen him with an unhappy expression during the last few days.'

'Do you know him then?'

'I see him often in the Bois de Boulogne,' the young woman replied evasively.

'Poor chap. Please be kind to him. Tell his beauty whom I strongly suspect of being one of your friends, to take pity on him.'

'I cannot do that, but I will ask you to give him a piece of good advice, which is to forget this adventure.'

'Oh, why so?'

'Because this love affair has no future.'

'Poof.'

'It is as I said: it seems their molecules lack the hooks to bond them together.'

'Oh, how strange. Has Madame Granada a boudoir dedicated to Venus, as well?'

'Not as far as I know. I know Granada and I do not think she is one of those who loves pleasures obtained by virile force pure and simple.'

'Is she a primitive woman?'

'Yes, deep down, but one on whom the influence of civilisation can be felt.'

'Periwinkle, my darling, could we go to bed?'

'No, it's too late: I shall miss my last train.'

'What, you are leaving tonight?'

'Yes.'

'Do you live in the country near Paris?'

'I live in Paris, China, Chicago, and in Calcutta, my good friend – it is no concern of yours.'

161

'You are quite right. But you must admit that this situation is intriguing. However, I don't want to nag you, my little darling, so I shall leave. When shall I see you again?'

'In five or six days' time.'

'Oh, please be more precise because I fear the same fate as Paliseul's.'

'Have no fears on that score: I have no thought of being so cruel and, to prove it to you, I shall say Thursday.'

'Good, let it be Thursday then.'

Periwinkle rang. Félicité appeared and when Maxence had give the last kiss to his gentle friend he followed her, more and more anxious to discover the mystery of pretty Periwinkle.

'Dear Félicité,' he said to her as they crossed the large hall of the house, 'would you give me the great pleasure of telling me where I could find an album of watercolours similar to that on the table of your mistress's boudoir?' And, as he spoke, Maxence slipped five louis into the servant's hand.

'No, sir,' Félicité said with great deliberation, 'but I can have one made for you for which you need not pay in advance: you are one of those whose credit is good and, as for me, I am not one to betray her mistress for money.'

Maxence, a little disconcerted, put his money back in his waistcoat pocket and, after travelling round Paris for a long time beside his black companion, suddenly found himself within a stone's throw of the Circle of Artichokes. The vehicle stopped to allow him to alight and he had been on the pavement for a few seconds watching the carriage which had brought him rapidly disappear towards the Champs Elysées, when he was roughly shaken by Paliseul who said to him in an extremely agitated tone of voice:

'That was the sphinx's carriage. I saw it with my own eyes, you cannot deny it.'

'No, I shan't, my dear fellow. I have just passed some hours in the enchanted nest of Madame Periwinkle.'

'Let's follow the vehicle.'

'Don't be silly. If we tried to follow those horses in a hackney cab, we would lose them in just a few minutes.'

'That's true, but tell me have you unravelled the mystery?'

'No.'

'What, you know nothing more?'

'Well, yes, at least I think I know something more: first of all they are friends, Granada and Periwinkle. Then, our beauties live in the country and only spend part of their time in Paris. All the same, we meet them in the houses we visit or at least the ones they frequent must be in close contact with the ones we do, because they know all about our doings.'

'And you haven't heard from Periwinkle whether Granada thinks about me?'

'Well, I have got a message to you from her.'

'And you say nothing. Quick, speak up.'

'My friend, don't get excited and don't expect too much.'

'Why?'

'Because I have been asked to advise you to forget all about an evening which will have no morrow.'

'Really? And what is the reason for this decision?'

'A lack of hooked molecules, it appears. You are dealing with a woman who loves the solid and substantial, and it appears that you were not brilliant, because she wants no repetition of your little feast.'

'All the same,' Paliseul said with a piqued expression.

'You can say "all the same" as long as you like but I am telling you the truth and you would be ill-advised to hold it against me, because I am merely acting as a faithful messenger.'

'No doubt, you are going to boast of your success and mock my failure in the circle.'

'No, my dear fellow, neither the one nor the other. The women who entertained us are not of the type who have nothing to lose, and it would be unworthy of gentlemen to make their moments of madness the subject of compromising talk; moreover, it would be an unfriendly act towards you to gossip about the capricious inconstancy of a woman who has turned against you. Don't worry about me and, to reassure you completely, I shan't even go up to the Artichokes.'

'Forgive me this slight suspicion, my dear Maxence, and don't trouble yourself about me. Go up and see our friends, by all means: I have every confidence in your word.'

'I don't doubt it, but I must confess to you that my adventures with Madame Periwinkle have shaken my nerve a little and all I want is a glass of punch and then to get back to my lodgings. Would you like to accompany me to my place?'

'With pleasure.'

Paliseul and Maxence went their way.

CHAPTER SEVEN

'Well, darling sister,' Florentine asked Julia when the two of them were at luncheon the following day and the servants had withdrawn, 'what happened yesterday? Why did you ask me to leave for Paris early?'

'Because of a rather strange adventure.' Julia told her sister the details of her visit to the art gallery, of the evening she had spent with Michel and the promise she had made him to go and see him in his studio.

'Where might this lead? Be careful, this young Michel has seen you without a mask and he may recognise you.'

'I don't believe he has any connection with the people we know. All the same I don't disagree with you, but I don't know what attraction it is that makes me want to follow this adventure to the very end. There is something original and natural in Monsieur Lompret which I find seductive. His language is not that of the people we know and he lives at ease in the world of ideas, which we know about only from novels. He has a way of looking at love which presents that sentiment in a new light; in short, I certainly don't love him yet, but he has captured my imagination in such a way that I can think of nothing but him.'

'Well, that's it, then,' Madame Vaudrez said and

she lifted her finger up to the level of her forehead as a sign of warning.

'No, no,' the young woman countered with an impatient gesture. 'And you?', she asked. 'What did you do with Maxence?'

'I have discovered an unknown world, my darling, and I have certainly spent a little while on one of the most beautiful islands in the middle of the river of tenderness hitherto unexplored, at least by me.'

'As unfamiliar as that?'

'Yes, until now I have only seen it through a telescope, which you must admit gives a much less clear idea of places than an actual visit.'

'I agree, but tell me: what did he do to you on that island of yours?'

'Well, basically nothing particularly different from what you initiated me into, but his artistic execution was out of this world, to which must be added such details as the accompaniment of a moustache and his masculine outpourings which put the whole thing on a different level of joy. You see, a man who is able to caress like a woman has great natural advantages over her.'

'You think so?'

'Since yesterday I am sure of it.'

'So I have been eclipsed?'

'Oh no, my darling, I shall be ready for you whenever you like.'

'From the point of view of my own personal pleasure, I shall not ask you for anything, my love, because I appreciate such refinements, which I confess I don't have the time to savour, less than you. My blood seethes too much under ardent caresses. Then my being becomes intoxicated without the need of stimulants. You see, I feel very strongly that the day I am loved by someone to whom I am drawn both morally and physically — that, that day, I shall again taste complete happiness, which I believed I would never know again.'

'And you will take off your mask?'

'I don't know what I shall do. Tell me the truth, doesn't the mask begin to impede you in your amorous exploits?'

'A little.'

'Be careful!'

'Don't worry. But tell me, my prudent mother, did you ask Dorothy to find out a little about your Michelangelo before becoming his Fornarina?'

'No, no,' Julia said with a gesture of impatience. 'I don't want anyone to interfere with this chapter of my novel for fear it may lose some of its freshness.'

Florentine burst into laughter and got up from the table to avoid her sister's anger, the first symptoms of which were beginning to show in Madame de Corriero's eyes. She seized Cherubino and took him into the garden where for an hour mother and son played together.

Julia had gone back to her room, stretched out on a *chaise longue*, where she smoked a cigarette idly, following with her eyes the path of the smoke rising in great billows and later vanishing in space.

'How many things in life are ephemeral,' she thought. Then her thoughts took another tack, and she asked herself what would be the consequences of this acquaintance made in the gallery, and of the luncheon they had planned.

'Florentine is obviously right,' she said to herself, 'but she jars on me. I feel myself drawn to this unknown creature by a bizarre and incomprehensible attraction. His look seems to see beyond the earth, his harmonious voice expresses his thoughts in such

167

a clear and fine way; everything and nothing about him captivates me. I shall go to him. Yes, I will.'

This resolution brought serenity back to her spirit and so the young woman rejoined her sister and tried with a few caresses to overcome the small breach brought about by her brusqueness earlier on. This was quickly achieved.

All day, in spite of the decision she had taken, she remained thoughtful. Cherubino was called in to help and heaped a thousand caresses upon her. The child, who only wanted to play, adored his aunt that evening even more than usually.

Ungrateful little aunt! In spite of all his efforts, it was with a sigh of relief that she took the road to Paris because she was in a hurry to get back home and to prepare for the next day.

'I mustn't look like a little fool,' she said to herself, 'these artists are different from us. Nonsense, the main thing is to remain natural and not to try and imitate the frog blowing itself up to match the bull. He would not be fooled and I would lose what little personal worth I might have. Let me be a woman, let me be myself, let me ask him humbly to initiate me into the holy of holies of art.'

It was as a result of these sensible reflections that Madame de Corriero next morning instructed her lady's maid to get ready her grey suede outfit with steel buttons, very simple, all in one colour, the bodice fitting tightly over a skirt of soft tulled silk of the same shade, decorated at the neck by a bouquet of roses.

A hat, in the shape of a snail with feathers, and a very simple coat would complete her exquisitely simple costume.

She also thought about the means of transport she would use to go to Monsieur Lompret's and ended up by falling asleep thinking of Michel.

CHAPTER EIGHT

Madame de Corriero's heart was beating fast when next day she knocked at the door of the small house belonging to Michel Lompret. Good heavens! the reader might say – an artist in his own furnished flat is a rare phenomenon, but a house of his own, that's going too far!

All the same, dear reader, this is how it was. There was a time when art seemed to be a priesthood and its disciples devoted the purest part of their souls and their physical strength to it, so that, in general, they died in poverty after a life of hardship. In our day, things are no longer like that. The wings of enthusiasm have been clipped and nothing is done to excess. The painter produces, the sculptor carves blocks of marble, the musician combines harmonies, not in obedience to an impulse which makes him pour out the overabundance of his soul but to make money. People no longer aim for what is beautiful: they prefer what is saleable. People no longer cultivate those charming eccentricities which cost an arm and a leg. Careful attention is paid to the ledger. An artist has become a merchant trading in the products of his art, with the same shrewdness as a grocer dealing in sugar and molasses. This was not entirely the case with Michel Lompret. His father had left him a tidy fortune and he pursued his art in the charming little house which he had built and where he had established himself with an old solider, a former batman of the General's.

Pegleg acted as his cook, valet and sometimes even nurse.

Julia had to make complicated arrangements in order to keep secret where she was going. The life of a young woman with a domestic staff and a carriage is difficult to keep concealed. More than one great lady owes the integrity of her virtue to the difficulty of putting into practice the plans she may have made to undermine it. Madame went out in a hackney cab instead of giving instructions for the horses to be harnessed. Why? Because it is rare for her not to be followed furtively. If she uses a carriage, the coachman and the footmen have to become her confidants and accomplices.

Julia devised an excellent plan for keeping her secret. She pretended to want to be taken to the Gare du Nord and gave orders that she was to be met there in the evening. When the vehicle had departed, she went towards the arrival platforms and huddled into a hackney cab which took her to the heights of Montmartre without her being seen by anyone.

Michel's door did not remain closed to her for long. The cab had hardly stopped, when the gate clanked on its hinges and the old servant approached.

'If Madame would have the goodness to come in,' he said, 'I shall settle with the driver.'

Having said this, Pegleg gave the visitor a look that was at first curious and then approving, the effect of which was quite comical. Julia quickly got to the staircase, at the bottom of which she found two arms stretched out to receive her and where, without having had time to protect herself against it, she was given a tender kiss.

'Well, well,' she said, half laughing and half protesting.

'My lovely friend, I am so happy you have kept your word that it seems to me, a small degree of effusiveness is not out of place. In any case here we are not in a drawing-room; we are artists in our own home, free from all the shackles of convention. So, my dear Sauvageonne, no unnecessary inhibitions, no reserve, let us love each other as nature tells us to and let us, like the wise, take time by the forelock and people for what they are. Don't you agree?'

'Yes, only it seems to me that if, instead of being a weak woman, I were a man the situation would be simpler.'

'I don't believe it.'

'Nevertheless, it is so and I shall have a man's suit made for me in order to come and see you. Give me the address of your tailor.'

'I can do better than that. If you wish, Pegleg will go and see him after lunch, and you will be able to give him his orders without his knowing who you are. It will be charming. We shall walk about and travel like that because, you see, ever since the day before yesterday my spirit has taken the bit between the teeth and has not stopped making endless plans.'

'What kind of plans?'

'I shall tell you, but first of all come into the sanctuary and take off your hat and coat.'

They went into the artist's large studio. It was decorated tastefully and even luxuriously as is usual with a home in which the greater part of one's life is lived. The old furniture, the rare tapestries, the china, the precious bibelots were combined with discrimination. The plants and flowers, put there perhaps specially for the occasion, also produced a very charming effect.

In the middle of the room, a small deliciously laid and decorated table, with two places facing each other, made a most attractive sight.

'My bedroom is through there,' Michel said raising a vertically sliding door 'and my dressing-room is over there. Now, dear Madame, make yourself at home and your very humble servant will present his homage to you.'

Everything was well-ordered in Michel's home, nothing suggested the untidy confusion sometimes found in artists' houses. Julia put her coat on the divan and showed herself in the splendour of her figure, which was both slender and opulent, shown off to perfection by her tight-fitting suede dress. She raised her arms to remove the elastic of her hat but Michel did not give her the time to do that and, as the hat no longer covered a ravishing pink ear, he bestowed a greedy kiss upon it.

'Again,' Julia said wagging an admonitory finger at him 'I shall get cross.'

'Why, what wrong have I done?'

'You seem to me to have a very easy manner.'

'Oh, my entire catechism can be summed up in these words: do unto others as you would be done to yourself, or in that other adage: love each other. So I shall be the happiest of men if you would return to me the kiss I have just given you. As for the second commandment of my decalogue, I very much fear I might overdo putting it into practice, at least as far as you are concerned.'

'What would be the harm in that, I would ask in my turn?'

'If you can't see it, I shall absolve myself.'

'Go in peace, my son, and sin no more.'

'My friend, what you are ordering me to do here is rather difficult.'

'Why?'

'Because I do not feel at peace at all . . .'

'Luncheon is served, sir,' Pegleg announced.

Michel took the young woman's arm and led his visitor to the table.

'It's nice to have lunch like that *à deux*.'

'Isn't it? The oysters will seem all the better for it. As for me, this morning I see a heavenly light in my studio and life seems to me to be woven in pink and blue with hints of tender green here and there.

Ah, woman, the beloved woman, how much happiness she can give us but also how much pain, and, unfortunately, she is often cruel.'

'The beloved woman can do all that, yes, but in general has a woman so much influence on a man?'

'Oh yes, but do not ask me any more, because our conversation will immediately get into paths that are too personal. I want – as I told you, my beloved, – to have your soul, but I want it to come to me willingly; I don't want to capture it on the sly. I think I can recognise in you the sacred flame of artists and I would like to see it illuminate everything around our hearts.'

'It seems to me, dear Michel, that you are making me a declaration.'

'No, I am merely expressing my thoughts . . . But in doing so, I have forgotten to notice that you are not eating. Look at those little shells which seem to be begging for the privilege of being consumed by you.'

Michel pushed the plate of oysters in the direction of the young woman, who selected some. The luncheon proceeded gaily. Fried smelt and young partridge with truffles followed the oysters. The Sauterne was replaced by a Saint Julien and, finally,

173

the joyful detonation of a Moët et Chandon cork re-echoed in the studio.

The table companions were young, good-looking, happy and love was knocking at the door, so how could they fail to agree with Pangloss that all was for the best in the best of possible worlds? By the time they got to the dessert, a fair degree of intimacy had been established.

The young woman and her lover were thinking out loud, saying everything that came into their heads and Michel found with enormous pleasure that his personal impressions were echoed by his neighbour, and that she had all the intellectual qualities needed to become the companion of an artist. Pegleg served discreetly and only came in when summoned. He did not seem in the slightest bit surprised when Michel instructed him to put the coffee next to the divan on a little Japanese table. Once the after-dinner coffee had been served and the cigarette-box put out on the table, he retired, announcing to his Master that he was going on the errand he had been sent on, that is, to find the tailor.

'Very good, my dear chap,' Michel said, 'go along and don't forget to bring the little model who came yesterday, you know, the dark one.'

A little model – a brunette! . . . there is nothing extraordinary in those words because it is quite natural that an artist should receive models in his studio. All the same they made a painful impression on Julia. A cloud darkened her face and Michel noticed.

'What is the matter, my lovely Sauvageonne?' he asked. 'Why the sudden gloomy and severe look?'

Without making the effort to consider what her words would reveal, Julia replied with a question:

'Who is this model?'

Michel was too much a man of the world to fail to understand the import of this speech from a woman like Madame de Corriero, but he was also too sophisticated to give any hint that he had understood what it meant.

'It's a little girl of sixteen whom I found last night begging at the bottom of the rue des Martyrs. She is a pretty gypsy type and I am making a sketch of her; I'll show it to you if you will let me.'

Julia recovered her equanimity, sat down on the divan and prepared to pour the coffee.

'It is delicious to have a cup of coffee poured by a dainty hand like this,' said Michel who, as he took the cup being offered him, kissed the long, slender fingers of Madame de Corriero's hand.

'Now then, gently; how frisky this young man is — he is making me spill my coffee.'

'Frisky why — not at all. See how good I am: I am putting my cup next to yours and am sitting down beside you. We shall enjoy our coffee more when we are sitting comfortably like this.'

Michel sat on the divan, gallantly put his arm round his neighbour's waist, and, as she did not protest, drew to his chest the charming creature with whom he was taken more and more.

Julia, for her part, was more moved than she had expected when she came and yielded to the influence of the atmosphere in which she found herself: Michel's vibrant voice, the theories he talked about and also the indescribable well-being, which an excellent luncheon produced. She did not feel any particular ardour but a delightful sense of langour invaded her entire being.

'Sauvageonne, you are beautiful, beautiful,' the young man murmured.

Sauvageonne did not reply but with Michel's hand

on her heart she felt the vibrations of her crazed heartbeat.

'You know my darling, that the sight of the beautiful intoxicates the artist more than wine. Can you not feel that the whole of my being is going out towards you. Can you not understand that at this moment I am playing for high stakes – happiness or misery. Don't be flirtatious . . . Be the true woman that I feel you to be, true of heart, true of soul, true in her senses, one who does not believe herself to be obliged all the time to conceal her feelings. Tell me the truth, do you feel yourself attracted to me?'

The young woman dropped her head on to her neighbour's shoulder – all the reply she gave him. Michel felt a violent emotion in his heart. He paled, placed his lips on Julia's and for a long time they gradually drank in each other's breath. When this fiery kiss had come to an end, neither of them had any more doubts and if they had been less engrossed in their own feelings, they might have seen in the middle of the studio the little God of love no longer, as before, hidden behind the curtain but out in the open and clapping his hands in glee as he looked at them.

They were oblivious of the past and the future. They were overcome by intense intoxication. Their lips became mute and it was in an inarticulate murmur that Michel said, 'I love you, be mine,' and it was almost automatically that he undid the young woman's bodice and bared her shoulders. A scented wave, consisting of an enticing mixture of feminine odours and those produced by the perfumer's art, rose to his head and drove away his pallor. Then the blood which had rushed to his head, drained away again; he became pale once more; his soul had just been drunk and now it was the turn of his senses. He bent over the white shoulders which emerged from the gray framework of the dress and devoured them with kisses, not a glutton's brutal kisses but the caresses of a gourmet. While kissing her, he acted: his hands quickly undid the buckles of the little white satin belt round her waist.

Julia made a gesture of protest but this was her last concession to convention. Michel, pressing her more energetically, carried the day.

Her corset fell to the floor as did her dress. The young man, like the disgarded garments, slipped to the floor and, without ceasing to embrace Madame de Corriero's waist with one hand, he took off her boots and her grey silk stockings with the other; then he covered those bared feet and legs with passionate kisses.

Soon he gave his caresses an upward direction and became bolder. The young woman's thighs were silhouetted under the cambric of her shift, and he gently stroked them with his fine, fair beard. Half recumbent on the cushions, Julia remained motionless as if she had swooned and only the light tremors running up and down her skin revealed the intensity of her sensations. Michel turned her back a little and made himself a collar of her legs and, with a movement that was as rapid as it was discreet, undid the buttons of some of his garments the presence of which seemed to him inappropriate. The movement necessary to put Madame de Corriero's legs on his shoulders resulted in her shift moving upwards. Two rounded and firm thighs appeared and the little hillock of love surrounded by a curly fleece was happily displayed to Michel. The state of violent over-excitement in which the young man found himself deprived him of his mastery over himself; all the same it was at first only his lips which saluted the treasures yielded up to him and only when he heard Julia murmur 'come . . . come . . . with you . . . I want . . . with you . . . ,' did he give himself up to the transports which his entire being demanded.

There are moments in life which cannot be described: they must be experienced to be understood for it would be an error to suppose that they are given to all to enjoy. Many speak of them but few have known them. May those who have been favoured by good fortune remember!

Michel Lompret and Madame de Corriero were among the elect so the ecstasy that followed lasted a long time. The thought of separating their two bodies, united by an amorous spasm, did not occur to them. It was on this divan still linked together as closely as possible, that they recovered their senses and that in the middle of a kiss they said simultaneously to each other, 'I love you.'

CHAPTER NINE

Everything in this world comes to an end. Hours had passed. Pegleg had returned from his shopping expedition and knocked at the studio door in vain. He then peeped through the keyhole and retired to the kitchen, saying to himself, 'Good Lord, how good it is to be young and beautiful like those two there. Still I've had my day – only it's a long time ago.' With that resigned philosophical reflection, the old servant began to prepare tea, which he supposed they would ask him for, at about five.

This, in effect, was what happened. A ring at the tradesmen's entrance bell recalled our lovers to the realities of life.

'Pegleg must have gone out,' Michel said, 'who can that be?' He looked out into the street from one of the studio windows. It was the tailor. Pegleg, who was not out, opened the door to him and invited him to wait as the Master was very busy at the moment.

'Darling, it's the tailor,' Michel said, 'do you still want to be dressed like a man to be more at ease in my presence?'

'Oh no,' she said, putting her arm round Michel's neck. 'Now I would die of shame in front of that man if he came in. In any case,' she said boldly, 'at this moment I intend to be a woman and more of a woman than ever.'

'It is certain that you would lose by the change and I can't see what good having yourself measured for a man's suit would do now.'

'Send him away, then.'

'Right, retire to my bedroom and I shall ring for my Caleb.'

Julia got up. Michel collected up her garments scattered all over the carpet and took them to the room next door where, still quite confused, she had taken refuge. He pressed her tenderly in his arms and then left her to herself.

At the first ring of the bell, Pegleg roused himself. You could hear the tock-tock of his wooden leg on the wooden floor and he then presented himself at the door of the studio with a discreet expression which irritated Michel.

'Who is in the hall?' he asked gruffly.

'The tailor.'

'Oh well, tell him that I have changed my mind and that he can go again. You can also tell him that he can make me a smart travelling suit, so that he won't have been troubled for nothing.'

'That's all right; we can get rid of him without that,' the old servant mumbled as he turned on his heels.

When he came back, he said, 'Oh, I forgot to tell you that I could not find the model.'

'Let her go to hell; I don't give a damn.'

'The devil,' Pegleg thought. 'He certainly seems to have taken a fancy to this one. There is no doubt that she is a tasty piece. If she goes to it with spirit once more soon, it'll make me feel all the younger.'

'Make some afternoon tea, old chap, will you?' Michel said. 'Bring it to us when it's ready.'

'It will take half an hour.'

'That's good, go ahead,' Michel said turning his back.

The bedroom door consisted only of a blind of thick fabric and the dressing-room also was divided off by a large Chinese and very heavy screen which, when lowered, cut it off from the studio. Julia was unaware of the details of this combination and took her clothes into the dressing-room where she set about repairing the disorders in her dress caused by the amorous skirmishes in which she had just participated.

Having no suspicion that she could be seen, the young woman put a tub in the middle of the room, filled it with scented water, let down her shift and, arming herself with a large sponge, surrendered to the delights of prolonged ablutions. Michel in the middle of his studio watched this charming scene and the artist in him gained the upper hand. He saw the young woman untie her long hair, then put it up gracefully, pick up her garments one by one and, had she been less prompt in getting dressed, he would, very likely, have been tempted to take up his brushes. Julia, however, was too quick for him. A few minutes later, a little pale but smiling, she rejoined him. Their hands linked.

'My dearly beloved, have you found everything that you wanted, in my bachelor's quarters?'

'Yes, everything, even . . . I was morally dead when I came but I shall be leaving full of hope and love.'

'You will be leaving? Do we have to part?'

'Yes, alas, but we will meet again very soon.'

'My darling, a week ago we did not know each other and now we are united. I feel myself to be yours and I think of you as mine without reservations. All the same, I don't know what name to give you. Sauvageonne might have been suitable under the verdure of Montmorency but do you still think it suitable now?'

'No,' Julia said, becoming serious, 'I shall confide in you completely and I shall do so without fear.' She kissed Monsieur Lompret. 'To all the world I am Madame de Corriero and to you – Julia.'

At that moment all the resolutions made and all the effort and expense of decorating the house in the rue Charles V were forgotten. A thunderbolt of love has passed through there. Julia loved, she loved truly and she felt no sentiments other than those of unheard of voluptuousness, which made her yield herself up entirely with all her soul and all her passion, as if she were one body and soul with the man who once again made her heart beat faster and her senses tremble.

'Oh, my Julia, you will never regret having had faith in my honour and the care of your own will from now on be my chief concern. I shall guard it jealously, you may be certain. But, surely, we don't have to part today?'

'I have given orders that I am to be met at the Gare du Nord at ten o'clock tonight. I had intended to dine with my sister in the country and not to return by rail to my house until that time.'

'Let's put into practice only the second part of the programme and let us dine together.'

'I should be delighted.'

'That's agreed then, but I can hear Pegleg bringing us tea.'

Pegleg glanced at Madame de Corriero and saw that she was as correctly dressed as if she had emerged from the hands of her lady's maid; she was now making polite conversation with his master.

He said to himself, 'These society people are really something. Truly, if I had not seen them at it just now, I might have believed . . . still if it amuses them to act like that, . . . it's none of my business.'

And Pegleg, like the sensible man he was, withdrew with a shrug of his shoulders.

When Michel and Madame de Corriero were well into nibbling biscuits and sipping Malaga wine, the young painter felt the need for confidences and, between two kisses, he asked Julia:

'Why, darling, did you say just now that when you arrived here you were dead morally? Weren't you happy?'

'In the eyes of the world, I lacked for nothing but happiness is a strange plant: it grows where it wants to and, for no apparent reason, it can be seen to flourish in poor soil and not to blossom where human wisdom would expect it to.'

'Would you like to open your soul to me, my friend? I am worthy of your confidences, believe me. Without a doubt you have loved and suffered and then you did not want to believe in happiness any longer, so your little heart languished.'

'More or less.'

'Well, since I have guessed, fill in the details a little.'

'You are inquisitive.'

'No, not inquisitive; just a good chap who feels he has just offered up to you his entire life and who would suffer if he felt there was the slightest vestige of mistrust between your soul and his.'

'In that case, you shall be satisfied and we will rake over the ashes of the past even at the risk of some spark flaring up, but on one condition: you must make yourself responsible for preventing any conflagrations and, if these confidences should cause me pain, you will have to cure it.'

'Oh, I don't want as many details as that. Just

tell me whether your husband was young or old and whether you loved him.'

'He was seventy-eight.'

'Seventy-eight!' The words froze Michel's heart. So this beautiful creature gave herself up to an old man probably for material gain. 'Perhaps she was poor,' he said to himself to excuse her, but it still left behind a painful impression, of which Julia was aware, because she added:

'He died two years ago and I shall always venerate his memory for he was the most devoted and most affectionate father that one could wish for.'

'Father, did you say?'

'Yes, father,' Julia replied stressing the word.

'Nothing more?'

'Nothing at all.'

Suddenly she understood; she read Michel's heart like an open book.

'Oh,' she said, 'you thought that ... what an unpleasant thought – it wounds me.'

'Why, my darling?'

'You supposed that I gave myself to my husband.'

'Well, dear lady, surely it is not unreasonable to think that when a man gets married it is to have a wife.'

'That was not Monsieur de Corriero's motive at all. Listen to my story because I see that otherwise you will not fail to go astray in your opinion of me. Oh, fie on you!'

'My dear child, the best way of avoiding misunderstandings between us is to be perfectly frank.'

'What, a general confession?'

'Yes, and I promise absolution to my pretty penitent in advance. Sit down there close to me, my daughter, and tell me how it is that, in spite of the fact that your husband was nothing but a father to you, you no longer possess that which distinguishes the girl from the woman.'

'I shall tell you and confess. But, seriously, I want you to know me well, because I too feel that I have just passed an hour which will have a decisive influence in my life.'

'Dearly beloved, I hear you, and if you have any weaknesses to reproach yourself with, you can count on my indulgence.'

'You will confess, too?'

'In all sincerity.'

The young woman got on to her knees close to Michel, who wanted to object but finally they agreed on a compromise. Julia remained on her knees between the legs of her confessor so that his thighs could serve as an elbow-rest for her, and she could hide her face in his lap. In this position she told him the story of her life, her making her home with Aunt Briquart, the love of Viscount Saski, the way in which she gave herself to him without being his wife so as to save him from financial disaster and the betrayal with which her trust was rewarded. She told him about her sorrows and of the devotion of Don José de Corriero; in short, she told him everything except the episode with Paliseul, which she passed over in silence.

'And what have you been doing these past two years?'

'For the last two years,' Julia replied evasively 'I was waiting for my heart to heal and for it to be resurrected by love, a resurrection that has just come about. So now I am singing Hallelujah . . . there it is, Father, that is all I have to confess. If some details have escaped me, we shall mention them in future conversations.'

'On the contrary, we shall forget them altogether from now on.'

'Must I now say "Mea culpa, mea maxima culpa?" '

'No, my dear child because you are not blameworthy. You loved, you had faith . . . if you had felt mistrust in your heart you would not have loved truly. Go in peace! We must never blush for our entanglements if they result from the commands of love, our all-powerful master. Not only do I absolve you in my heart but I feel my estimation and affection for you growing. You are truly the woman of my dreams and we shall be happy. May the peace of the Lord accompany you, my daughter.' Michel re-inforced his words with a tender kiss.

'And now it is your turn,' Julia said and stood up.

Michel did not have anything very interesting to confess. He had been in love, he had had mistresses, but he had never really loved, and he was well aware now of how different everything that had gone before was from his present feelings. He spoke of his childhood, of his artistic vocation and of his loves. He embraced his confessor a great deal and finished up by going out with her arm in arm, taking her to dine in a small restaurant: Julia was enchanted.

At ten o'clock he escorted her to the Gare du Nord, where he left her by the departure platforms and pretended to go home, but instead he followed her from a distance until he saw her get into her carriage in front of the arrival platforms. Then, with very small steps, he started to wander along the boulevard, recovering his self-possession and recollecting every small detail of the day and of the confidences he had heard. He got back home at two o'clock in the morning, invaded by a sense of immense happiness and enormous warmth, of the kind that the surprises

that fate sometimes has in store for us may bruise but
the memory of which is never erased.

CHAPTER TEN

'Where shall we meet?' Michel had asked when shaking his friend's hand.

'Well, the first time at my place when I hold my At Home.'

'So be it, but that's not enough.'

'Certainly not; so if you wish to join me the day after tomorrow opposite the Jean-Jacques Hermitage in the Forest of Montmorency, you'll be welcome.'

'That's all right if it's fine but what if it's raining?'

'In that case, at your place; just wait for me.'

On the appointed day Michel wanted it to rain down in sheets but nothing of the kind happened. The sun rose radiantly.

'Fool of a sun which understands nothing,' the young man said to it.

Towards two o'clock, he was at the place indicated and saw Madame de Corriero arrive, gay and happy because of the fine weather, delighted to be meeting her friend again and to be walking with him in the sunshine.

Michel greatly enjoyed this walk although he would have preferred to see Julia behind closed doors. Unfortunately, he was not prepared for the surprises which Dame Nature had in store for him. Michel was a chaste boy as far as his everyday way of life was concerned. He was not attracted to women unless they were surrounded by at least some aura of romance and poetry. He very rarely took a beautiful young woman into his arms solely to satisfy his physical needs.

The result of this was that he accumulated large quantities of love fluid, which — when he loved, as was the case now — became the cause of violent perturbation. He noticed the effects of this when, with Madame de Corriero's hand in his, he bent over her to embrace her and she saw her eyes, shining with love, reflected in his.

'Julia, don't look at me like that.'

'Why not?'

'Because it will make me commit a crime.'

'What crime?'

'Don't ask me.'

'You frighten me, I want to know what crime this is.'

'I shall defy the rules of God, the walkers and the great trees and I will rape you on the first mossy bank we find.'

'Nonsense! You can't be as excited as all that.'

'Just check up on my condition.'

'Well, well. Look, there's a spring there, go and refresh yourself by drinking a mouthful of clear water and let us be serious.'

'Serious! Never! Good Lord, what would be the point of that? But rest assured, I don't like spoiling a good thing. But you must be nice and come back to Paris tonight.'

'To your place?'

'Yes.'

'And your servant, the venerable Pegleg, won't we be shocking him?'

'Pegleg? I shall bid him make himself scarce and also hold his tongue.'

'And if he saw me coming into your place at such an inappropriate hour, what would he think?'

'To explain your daytime visits, I shall start a portrait of you, which like Penelope's tapestry will never be finished.'

'But at night?'

'Julia, my love, we shall have to organise our existence because, if you truly love me, it can't go on like this.'

'If I love you! How wicked of you to doubt it.'

'Is it true, do you really love me?'

'But, of course, you great baby, and to prove it I shall do something very foolish.'

'You are very good.'

'I don't understand.'

'It's no good trying, my love; I haven't been able to understand myself for hours, so how could others manage?'

'Manage what?'

'Manage to understand me.'

'Well, I give up.'

'Tell me, when will I see you again alone?'

'Will you swear to me that, whatever happens, you will never remember on the morrow what happened the day before?'

'I swear it, but I affirm no less solemnly that I am very intrigued.'

'That's neither here nor there.'

'On the contrary.'

'Listen.'

'I'm all ears.'

'You will go back to Paris as you intended, you will pass the time as best you can and at nine o'clock precisely you will be in front of St Paul's church waiting for me.'

'You mean in the Marais?'

'Yes.'

'And afterwards?'

'Afterwards, you will see – or are you frightened by any chance?'

'Of not seeing you, yes.'

'I swear to you that I shall be there.'

'Well then I shall lay in a supply of patience and go.'

At nine o'clock Michel was looking at the church door when he saw a veiled and very simply-dressed woman alight from a cab and come to stand beside him. His heart did not deceive him: it was the one he was expecting. He went towards her quickly and stretched out a hand to her.

'I am on time, aren't I?'

'Like a chronometer.'

'Come,' she said.

She put her arm in Michel's and made him walk through several dark and dirty streets.

'Where are you taking me in this Godforsaken neck of the woods?'

'Here . . .'

Julia took a little key out of her pocket and used it to unlock a door leading to a garden of considerable size.

'Good Lord, it looks as if you have close connections in this place.'

'Very likely.'

They crossed the garden and were at the bottom of the large staircase of the house in the rue Charles V, as the reader has probably guessed. The old lamps were lit up, but not a servant was to be seen.

'We seem to have wandered into an enchanted palace,' Michel said.

'A palace of love.'

'Yes, it must be, since it is we who are there.'

191

Suddenly Dorothy loomed up before her mistress like a jack-in-the-box.

'Madame!' she exclaimed almost involuntarily.

'What is surprising about this? But I did not expect to find you here. Why are you?'

'On Madame Periwinkle's orders. Shall I withdraw?'

'No, light up my suite and help me undress.'

Dorothy disappeared and several moments later Michel Lompret was installed in Granada's boudoir where, however, he had the privilege of looking at her without her mask. He was too much of an artist not to be sensitive to the refinements of sensuality that were displayed in this suite. To say that he was happier there than in his own studio would not be true. It was something else. In the rue Charles V, he did not just find a languid young woman who allowed herself to be taken. Delightedly, he found one who gave herself, who cried out, who bit, who vibrated with passion, who was no stranger to any kind of voluptuousness and who knew how to savour it with transports of a kind to madden one's senses.

On the bearskin and in the great bed they had mad bouts of love. There was no fear of being disturbed. There were thick walls, great comfort, a charming woman, and there were no annoying trifles to rub the bloom off the situation. Who would have dared to say that Michel Lompret's lot was not enviable?

He had scarcely found himself alone with his friend, when Michel again felt the perturbation of which he complained in the forest and it must be admitted Julia was no less anxious to relive her recent experience.

If the moments she had passed with Monsieur de Paliseul had left her only with disagreeable memories, the hours she spent in Michel's arms did not have the same effect at all. There, she found again the physical sensations she had had in those of Gaston Saski and she was sure that in future they would surpass them in intensity, so she was in a hurry, now that the ice had been broken, to plunge into new Capuan delights.

Madame de Corriero made the lady's maid undress her quickly. Wrapped in a Chinese negligé, underneath which she wore nothing but her shift, with her bare feet protruding from her black velvet Turkish mules, she looked quite delicious. Michel took her in his arms and sat her on his knees. The appearance of the room they were in satisfied him that the woman he was with was far from innocent, so he put no restraint on the expression of his passion.

His hand quickly took an intimate path and wandered about the alabaster columns either side of the instrument of love. He lovingly pressed the soft fleece that surrounded it and lost no time in pulling up the fine fabric which concealed it from view. Then, feverishly taking off his clothes, he showed himself to the young woman in all the splendour of his manhood and responded to the cry of admiration that Julia let out by pressing her to his chest and lifting her up in his arms as if she were a child. He raised her clothing from behind and bared her two rounded buttocks which he covered with kisses before he put her on the bearskin in such a way as to be able to take her from behind, while with his agile finger placed on the clitoris, he directed her amorous contractions as he wished.

A double cry of pleasure resounded and the two beautiful lovers rolled on to the carpet. They swooned for a moment and thought they were dying; then they came back to life. Michel was mad with passion and his own over-excited nerves, so long deprived of exercise, tensed and untensed with delight. He understood the fiery temperament of the woman he was possessing and his amorous assaults multiplied and took on any number of forms. Lips to lips, chest to chest, they felt they were dying of happiness; her buttocks against his penis, Julia seemed to leave this earth. Languidly lying on her side, she experienced infinite delight. Finally, when nature could take no more their lips made themselves the auxiliaries of their happiness.

They no longer seemed quite human, the next day, when they awoke in the great bed where they had slept. However, a cold bath and a refreshing breakfast quickly overcame their fatigue. All the same, it took several days before they regained the power of their sensations. This period of calm was used to start the portrait and during those sessions the delights of the spirit and of the heart dominated those of the senses. It was then that the close bonds which only disaster could sever were forged.

Madame de Corriero had had to give some explanations to Dorothy so that the latter should not regard the newcomer in a poor light. This was all the more important as Julia had decided to take her dear Michel, whom she could not fool herself into thinking she could do without, to the *château* of La Bidouze.

La Bidouze is a very fine property situated on the banks of the river of the same name, in the department of the Basses-Pyrénées. It was part of the general's estate and it was Julia's intention to restore the old castle which had long been uninhabited and in which it had pleased her to spend several months of the year. Nothing was more natural than the presence of an artist in such surroundings.

Dorothy competently arranged all the details. To begin with, she was a little annoyed at not having been the go-between in this affair, because she enjoyed the comings and going of the sphinx but she consoled herself with the thought that this was a passing whim.

'Darling,' Michel said before leaving Madame de Corriero, 'where am I?'

'At my place.'

'At your place? But you live in the boulevard Saint-Michel.'

'Officially that is so but this is my "*buen retiro*".'

'So this is where the Pole . . . ?'

'Oh, no.'

'Then how come that this suite is so well organised to receive your chosen swains?'

Seeing the awkward direction the young man's thoughts were taking, Julia told him about her conversation with her sister, the scene that followed and Dorothy's advice.

'Terrible depraved little creatures,' he said.

'That's a profoundly false judgment, at least as far as I am concerned, and you should understand that I prefer natural to artificial pleasures.'

'That's true, but even if it were otherwise I would not regard it as a crime, because I cannot see any harm in preferring burgundy to claret; one weakens the body more than the other, but that is the only reproach I have to make of it. For the rest, your confidence moves me deeply and you can count on my absolute discretion.'

'It is because I have no doubts on that score that I beg Monsieur Lompret to remember that tomorrow is my day at home and that I shall be delighted to give him a cup of tea at my place.'

'Monsieur Lompret, Madame, will have the honour of paying his respects to you.'

The next day there was someone in Madame de Corriero's drawing room who was waiting impatiently for the visit of the young painter – Madame Vaudrez; so when Pierre announced Monsieur Lompret a little shiver of expectant curiosity went through her.

With the greatest grace in the world Michel greeted the mistress of the house and responded to the introductions which were made without a look or an intonation revealing any intimacy between himself and Madame de Corriero. When he had retired, the two sisters looked at each other.

'This is a young man as well brought up as Michelangelo,' Florentine said wickedly, 'and, by Jove, he is very handsome. Who knows, my dear sister,' she added 'perhaps chance has organised things better than all our little arrangements.'

'I believe so. However that may be, our little hideout in the rue Charles V was an excellent idea.'

'Wasn't it just, ladies?' Dorothy, who had come into the room that very moment, said. 'I am sure that from now on you won't be bored, thanks to it.'

'Quite right, faithful Dorothy, you have deserved well of your fatherland, so — as a reward — you are authorised to become the rightful owner of my grey dress and my granite-coloured hat.'

CHAPTER ELEVEN

'My love, I'm leaving for the Pyrenees next week,' Madame de Corriero said to Michel one morning.

'Leaving for the Pyrenees? Does that mean that we won't see each other any more?'

'Not see each other any more! What an idea! Aren't you as free as I am? Who is to stop you following me a fortnight later? I own an old castle in that part of the world. It is full of old pictures, so for all the world you will be the painter responsible for their restoration. For the rest, visitors will not disturb us much, because I am leaving with the express purpose of having a rest from *salon* life and I have no intention of resuming it in the country.'

'So that's agreed, then?'

'Perfectly. I shall go ahead next week.'

'Just as you wish, my lovely darling.'

While these arrangements were being made in Granada's bedroom, quite a serious event took place in Periwinkle's. Her mask slipped off and Maxence de Berny was stupefied to recognise Madame Vaudrez.

'It's you!'

'Yes it is. Chance is not so blind, after all; this stifling thing was beginning to be a nuisance. I hope you won't use this mishap to ruin my reputation.'

'What do you take me for? But there's one thing I will say – this is just another example of how women

197

love to complicate things. Don't you think I would
have been in a better position to protect your reputation without this sphinx nonsense and all these
mysteries?'

'How so?'

'It's obvious. The idlers of the Circle of Artichokes
are intrigued by my liaison and by Paliseul's adventure. Madame Granada and you have stirred up an
entire pack of bloodhounds that will sooner or later
find a clue, whereas if you had purely and simply
relied on the loyalty of two decent chaps you would
have run no danger.'

'But it was all such fun! And now that we are of
one mind, everything is all right. But what would
have happened if things had not worked out so well?'

'You mean if you had felt about me like Madame
Granada about Paliseul?'

Florentine nodded.

'Come to that, who is Madame Granada, the
brunette Andalusian lady?'

'Her secrets are not mine to divulge.'

'So be it. Now, little Periwinkle, as nothing I could
say about the situation would get us any further and
as it's no good crying over spilt milk, what I shall do
is to try and put the curious off the track.'

'How will you set about doing that?'

'Let me think about it.'

For a moment Maxence remained thoughtful.

'To whom is this house let?' he asked.

'Félicité.'

'Félicité? The Moor?'

'Yes.'

'And this estimable woman is no more black than
I am?'

'That's right. She is white, and a devoted servant
besides.'

'In whose service is she?'

'Granada's.'

'All right, I believe I've got it. The sphinx invites Paliseul to a rendezvous with Granada. I suggest to my fellow members of the Circle that they profit from this occasion to discover something of the beautiful stranger's secrets, while you arrange that we should find Paliseul in intimate contact with Félicité, who is the official tenant of the house.'

'That seems all right to me.'

'That's what we'll do then.'

'It will be an easy task.'

'Will you take it on?'

'Certainly.'

'All right, let's start tomorrow.'

Questions of detail and organisation were agreed and Maxence withdrew very thoughtfully, but not without first proving to Periwinkle that her confidence in him had not diminished his ardour towards her.

Two days later at about four o'clock Paliseul entered the rooms of the Circle with agitated footsteps.

'What's the matter?' Maxence asked him, 'you don't appear yourself today.'

'That's true but I am very happy.'

'Congratulations. May one ask the reason for the joy with which your soul is flooded.'

'The cruel Granada has relented.'

'No!' everyone exclaimed.

'It is as I said. Look, here is the invitation.'

'Paliseul, you know what you promised us?'

'Yes, and I won't deny it now.'

'That does you credit. So you are going to help us lift the mysterious veil behind which the secretive Mesdames Granada and Periwinkle are concealed?'

'One thing is certain,' Maxence said, but only to

himself. 'Madame Periwinkle is under my protection; woe to anyone who tries to harm her.'

'With pleasure, gentlemen,' Paliseul replied, 'only I don't know how to set about it.'

'Just tell us the time and place you have to meet the sphinx's carriage.'

'At nine o'clock in the Champs-Elysées by the tenth gaslight.'

'That's good enough.'

The sphinx's carriage arrived at the indicated hour and stopped at the agreed place. The negress put her head out of the window.

Paliseul got in, full of ardent expectations, and sat down beside her. The vehicle left at a trot without anyone noticing a modest cab drawn by a trotting horse, quite out of place between the shafts of this commonplace vehicle, moving off at the same time twenty paces behind. The smiling faces of Maxence de Berny, of Lyncent and of Melreuse were concealed behind its curtained windows.

Soon they reached the rue Charles V.

'Here it is,' the conspirators said, when they saw the vehicle stop in front of the gate of an old house. 'How shall we get in?'

'Periwinkle doesn't live here,' Maxence de Berny said.

'You think not?'

'I'm certain and I am willing to bet that Paliseul has told us a story dreamed up from beginning to end by his own imagination.'

'I don't believe it.'

'You will see that it's something like that. We have to surprise him and, to do that, we shall have to use a stratagem and bribe the doorkeeper of this respectable but also very sad-looking place.'

They rang and the door opened.

'We have a very urgent message,' Maxence, who had taken over the leadership of the expedition, said, 'for a friend of ours who has just gone up to see Madame Granada. Would you have the kindness to let him know that we are here.'

Saying this, he slipped a louis into the doorkeeper's hand.

The latter, who had been given his instructions, led the visitors up a convenient but very ordinary staircase, which had nothing artistic about it and the entry of which was at the bottom of a glazed-in courtyard.

'You can see it is nothing like the descriptions we have heard,' de Lyncent said.

'No,' Maxence replied, 'nor like anything I saw when I called on Periwinkle.'

The doorkeeper stopped on the first floor and there the gentlemen were ushered into a little drawing-room which looked very much like anybody else's. They were left there for a very long time, so long that the jibes began to fly and their patience was quite exhausted when the doorman at long last reappeared.

Without saying a word, he silently opened a low door covered by a curtain and motioned them to enter.

Obeying quickly, the three friends suddenly found themselves in a fine bedroom, this time very much like the one described by Paliseul. It was in semi-darkness which at first made the visitors hesitate. Two alarmed voices cried out and two bodies moved on the bed.

'I beg your pardon,' Maxence said, 'but I think we have been brought here by mistake.'

Suddenly the light of the lamp became brighter and every corner of the room was clearly lit up and, to their amazement, the group of friends saw – Paliseul girded for battle and tenderly holding a woman whose mask had slipped and revealed the slightly-altered features of Félicité Deschamps.

Paliseul shrank back.

'It would have been preferable, my dear friend, for our secret not to have been divulged,' Félicité said, 'but, now that it has happened, don't worry about it. I am sure that an appeal to these gentlemen's discretion will be enough to stop them talking about what they have seen, and I hope they will be kind enough to leave us now, so that we can resume our interrupted frolics.'

Saying this, Félicité with the most comic tenderness threw her arms round the young man's neck and drew him to herself.

He pushed her back roughly.

'Oh,' she said, apparently hurt by his manner, 'what is the meaning of this attitude and of the presence of these gentlemen in my house?'

'In *your* house? If I'm not mistaken you are the negress of Granada.'

'Granada or Seville, what difference does it make? Have I got a black skin to be taken for a Moor?'

Félicité, anxious to prove her European origins, let her slip slide down to below her breasts and lifted the bottom of it up to the small of her back.

'Have I the characteristics of that race?', she asked indignantly.

The Artichokes burst into laughter.

'It's a complete mystery to me,' Paliseul said.

'I don't know what mystifies you, sir,' Félicité replied 'but what I do know is that I am in my own house, that I have twice honoured you with my favours in this very room and that you ought to be grateful. Now, my little one,' she went on in the accents of the suburbs, 'I have had enough. Put on your trousers and go off with your friends, if they still claim that questionable honour, on which I do not compliment them.'

During this speech, Paliseul got up, dressed quickly and addressed the group that was mocking him.

'I shall follow you, gentlemen, because I must ask you how it happened that you should be in Madame's bedroom at this hour.'

'That's very simple. We wanted to speak to you. Madame has an incompetent servant who showed us in here.'

'There is the way out,' Félicité said, having by now put on a dressing gown.

She showed the visitors and Paliseul, who was very angry, a spiral staircase leading to the garden. There, they found the doorkeeper who took them a considerable way and ended up by opening a gate which gave on to an obscure lane.

When they were in the street, Maxence, Lyncent and Melreuse let out a great laugh.

'So that's her, that houri, that splendid star.' they said.

'You, you're a man of imagination, Paliseul, and a good deal of that commodity is needed to see exceptional charms in the proprietress of this enchanted palace. Your Granada, my good fellow, beats everything.'

'Come, come,' Maxence said in a good-natured tone, 'you are hardly fair; her bottom is still very fine. Admittedly, she is a little knock-kneed and her breasts require a few applications of ass's milk but, all in all, she wasn't bad.'

'I am going mad, I'm sure,' Paliseul said in a distraught voice.

'Not at all, my friend, not at all. Monsieur de la Palisse would tell you that you cannot distinguish features under a mask. Under the influence of all this mystification with the sphinx, etcetera, you saw marvels, where there was only a good lady past her prime, probably very rich, who despaired of making conquests with her face uncovered and so called to her aid a lot of tempting little tricks.'

'My poor Paliseul, you have been duped.'

'And you with Periwinkle?'

'Oh, no. In the first place, it was not in this house that I was received and, secondly, as I have seen her without a mask I know with whom I am dealing.'

'Without a mask?'

'Yes.'

'A courtesan? A woman of the *demi-monde?*'?

'You must allow me to remind you of the fundamental rule of a gentleman's catechism: "he who foregoes it, is a fool, but he who boasts of it is a bastard!" On this note, my good friends, I bid you good night. I leave you to comfort Paliseul, while I myself shall go to bed.'

Having assured himself that no-one was following him, he went back to the rue Charles V, where he found Periwinkle and Dorothy splitting their sides.

'Well,' they asked, 'was it well played?'

'Admirably. Dorothy was splendid and so natural. If you could only have seen, Periwinkle, with what self-assurance she exhibited her secret possessions to us. My compliments, Dorothy, on your splendid bottom.'

'Your Lordship pleases to jest.'

'Not at all, Dorothy, and — to prove that the sight of it dazzled me — here are ten louis which I am giving you for the pleasure I had in contemplating them.'

'Your Lordship is very good and at that price I shall be at his service any time he wishes.'

'Much obliged, Dorothy, but one mustn't overdo even the greatest pleasures.'

'And what is my lover saying now?'

'He is seriously wondering whether he shouldn't consult a psychiatrist.'

'Oh, what a marvellous story,' Florentine exclaimed, while at the same time dismissing Dorothy with a gesture.

The Artichokes discussed these events for a long time but they no longer sought the key of the mystery, which is just what Maxence de Berny had wanted.

Paliseul, who had become the butt of these gentlemen's jokes, thought it appropriate to lodge a bullet in the shoulder of one of them, which quietened the rest and, now that the mystery appeared to be solved, the aristocratic members of the Circle of Artichokes concentrated on other matters.

The incident was apparently closed, but in Paliseul's heart the fury of wounded pride continued to seethe and he vowed to take revenge on the person who had mystified and humiliated him so much.

CHAPTER TWELVE

The *château* of Bidouze is an old building dating back to the thirteenth century, archaeologists say. Constructed half-way up a small mountain, it dominates the river that gave it its name and looks like a huge nest huddled up in foliage in the midst of the tall trees all round it.

This ancient dwelling had belonged to the parents of Señor Corriero; it was there that they had come after their marriage, and there that Don José was brought up.

Apart from its picturesque exterior, the old *château* was in no way remarkable.

All the luxury its former owners put into it seemed to have gone into the interior. The great rooms were full of the finest old furniture, the walls were covered with valuable pictures and the bookshelves contained a large quantity of rare books for which a collector would have paid a fortune.

Generations of the same family succeeded each other in this dwelling, each one leaving behind it the quintessence of its artistic or scholarly aspirations. There were, it is true, some cobwebs here and there but they could quickly be swept away and a week's domestic work would have been ample to get the house very comfortably organised.

There Julia waited for her dear Michel, for whom

she nourished a violent passion, and she began to count the days till his arrival, when a letter from her beloved came, a letter full of tenderness but also of sadness. An old aunt, whom the painter loved, was dying and required his presence in Nîmes. Michel wrote telling Julia that he was leaving Paris that day but warning her that it would be some days before they could meet at La Bidouze.

This letter made Madame de Corriero sad. To console herself, she made some excursions round her property, in which she let herself be guided by the niece of the *château's* general handyman, a child of about fifteen who was very badly brought up. As her mother had died some days after she was born, nobody had seriously bothered about her.

Madame de Corriero had at once understood the girl's unfortunate situation and had undertaken to take her to Paris and give her a suitable education.

'I have no children,' she said. 'I am rich and I owe it to society to provide for the needs of some of the deprived.'

The guardian of the child was informed of her intentions and expressed great satisfaction.

'Oh Madame, what a great service you will be doing me in relieving me of the duty of looking after this child – I don't know what to do with her.'

'Is it is agreed, then? You hand over to me all authority over her?'

'Certainly and willingly.'

From that day on, Julia took great care of the child. She bought suitable clothes for her and the girl scarcely left her side.

One day, on their way back to the *château* they came across a handsome youth, of about sixteen who seemed to be very ill, lying by the roadside.

Madame de Corriero approached him.

'What is the matter with you?'

'I am hungry.'

'You are hungry, poor boy. Claire,' she said to her companion, 'give him your snack and go and find Dorothy. What is your name?' she asked the lad.

'Pedro.'

'Are you Spanish?'

'I believe so.'

'Where are your parents?'

'They are dead.'

'And where do you live?'

'Nowhere. I was put in a home but I hated it, so I ran away and crossed the frontier.'

'All by yourself?'

'Yes, I got by by begging, but I'm sure if you hadn't come I would have died.'

Madame de Corriero looked at him. He was a charming youth, well-built for his age, with a proud look, and he held promise of becoming a fine specimen of the type of man produced by the hot soil of Andalusia.

Dorothy arrived and was told about the incident. It was decided that Pedro should stay at La Bidouze for a few days.

Dorothy made him have a bath, the necessity of which was fairly obvious. A Spanish costume was made for him which suited him very well and Claire and he became the best of friends.

If Michel likes, Julia thought, he could do for Pedro what I am doing for Claire and later on when we are old we might marry these two young people off.

So before making a decision about the lad she waited for Monsieur Lompret's arrival.

Unfortunately, day followed day, bringing passionate letters from Nimes announcing that the aunt could not make up her mind either to get better or to pass on to a better world. Julia took her role as mother to Claire more and more seriously. She gave her lessons and taught her good manners; so her anger was understandable, when one afternoon, on a walk with Dorothy, she saw her ward on a grass bank with her legs in the air while young Pedro knelt in front of her and engaged in physiological researches with a studious expression, which a scholar of such matters might have adopted.

He was so engrossed in the subject that he did not notice the women's arrival.

Madame de Corriero made a sign to Dorothy and remained motionless for a moment. She then quickly approached the youngsters and restored Claire to a decent posture, as Pedro who seemed very embarrassed, tried to escape.

'Stay there, sir,' she said sternly. 'And you, young woman, tell me what you were doing, you brazen creature? You will get a lesson straight away which you won't forget in a hurry.'

'It was Pedro who wanted it,' the girl moaned.

'That's as it may be, but it's no reason to do his bidding. Dorothy will immediately administer punishment which will teach you to be less compliant when boys make demands of you.'

Julia broke off a few twigs from the bushes round the mass of neighbouring trees, gave them to her lady's maid and told her to raise the skirts of the culprit and cane her hard.

Dorothy without a moment's hesitation took Claire by the waist, raised up her petticoats and her shift, and with one hand laid her on the grass bank which had witnessed the crime, while with the other she conscientiously inflicted the punishment.

'Now,' Julia said, when the girl scrambled tearfully to her feet again 'see that it doesn't happen again.'

Claire immediately ran off to the house.

Meanwhile Pedro had been silent, while sheepishly standing on the spot where Julia's gesture had stopped him.

'As for you, I don't suppose you think that matters will be left as they are, and that you will get away without paying for what you have done. Claire was wrong to have yielded to your desires, but you are even guiltier than she in having asked her, so you will be punished, too. Dorothy, go and find the gardener.'

Dorothy picked up the flowers she had plucked in the greenhouse and went off.

'Why are you sending for Pierre?' Pedro asked gloomily.

'To punish you.'

'I shall strangle him if he touches me.'

'Oh, we'll see about that.'

'If I need to be punished,' the boy said, strangling a sob, 'it won't be by him; he isn't my father, he is only a servant.'

'Perhaps so, but as you have no father he will take his place.'

'That man will never touch me. As you took me on, I am like your child and you have the right to punish me. I'll take anything from your hand but not from him.'

'Well, all right – but, mind, you won't gain from the exchange. Let's get on with it and stop making such a fuss.'

Julia went up to the delinquent. Then, thinking that the sounds of the severe punishment she was determined to inflict would be heard from the garden, she decided it would be better to go indoors.

'Walk in front of me,' she said curtly.

Pedro did so slowly, and they went towards Madame de Corriero's dressing-room. In spite of his reluctance, he had to step into this charming retreat, the door of which Julia bolted. The room was at the end of a corridor which at that time was deserted. There nobody would be able to hear the protestations she expected.

In fact, while they were on the way to the place of torture, Pedro had put on a reasonably good face and all he did was to weep silently. But when he saw his protectress taking off her hat, rolling up her sleeves and pushing a large pouffe into the middle of the room, he understood that the critical moment was upon him and he threw himself on his knees asking for pardon with pitiful cries.

Julia was adamant: it would have been grossly unfair for Claire to be the only one to pay her debt to morality.

'If you don't submit, I shall send for Pierre,' she said in a merciless tone of voice.

And, as Pedro did not hurry to obey, Madame de Corriero quickly undid the hooks of the lad's trousers, which slid to his heels in spite of his efforts to keep them up.

She then quickly seized Master Pedro and reversed him with her left hand and lifted the shirt-tails which covered his fleshy parts. Then, with a white and soft but dry hand, she administered twenty hard slaps which brought a livid red colour to the culprit's buttocks and made him sob heart-rendingly.

Madame de Corriero was made breathless by the exercise she had just taken and sat down on a couch. She glanced at Pedro and was very surprised to see that, though he was upset and sobbing, he made no effort to dress. He held his painful buttocks in his two hands but did not move.

Her surprise grew even greater when she noticed something absolutely unexpected: Pedro, whose manliness was greater than his years or who was possibly older than he had announced, had an absolutely enormous erection.

'Well, well,' Julia thought, 'that's odd.'

'Get dressed,' she ordered the boy and let go of his shirt-tails, 'and from now on see to it that you behave in such a way that I shan't have to punish you again.'

This little scene remained etched in Madame de Corriero's mind and she continued to feel curious about it. Hardly a week had gone by when Pedro was again ordered to Madame's terrible dressing-room.

Pedro had stolen a pot of jam and persisted in energetically denying it even though Pierre had caught him red-handed.

'All right,' Madame de Corriero said when the complaint was brought to her, 'send him to me at about one o'clock.'

That was the time when the servants had their siesta and when Dorothy had her lunch.

Julia was very severe and very dignified when she questioned him at length about his double crime, larceny aggravated by lies. After that she indicated to him that he should prepare to receive the birch. The lad went very red but would not obey.

'Did you hear what I said?', Julia insisted.

'I daren't – I'm ashamed.'

'If you weren't ashamed of committing a crime, you must be courageous enough to take your punishment.'

Pedro had been called before his guardian so quickly, that he did not have enough time to think about it; also, he was very lightly dressed. It was not hard to deal with the few garments he had on and Julia very quickly bared his bottom. His shirt-tails and his twill smock were quickly tucked up in his leather belt. Then, Madame de Corriero took up the birch which had previously been prepared and

212

ordered Pedro to take up the traditional position for such a ceremony, but he persisted in remaining seated.

'Is that what you are going to beat me with?' he asked angrily and pointed to the hazel twigs which Julia held in her hand.

'Yes.'

'I won't . . . I won't!'

'I don't care, get into position.'

'No, you can hit me with your hand and I'll do as you say but I won't be birched like a dog.'

All the same, Pedro had to take the brutal caresses of the birch. In one movement, he was lifted off his seat and turned upside down in spite of his resistance.

As a result, he went red and pale with fury but nothing helped. Julia's left hand on the small of his back held him on the pouffe over which she had bent him with his bottom in the air, and his furious kicks reached only the wall and did nothing to prevent the dreaded twigs from performing their task. They were raised and lowered for a relatively long period but it looked as if this was done with a light hand because Pedro's protuberances were scarcely marked by any weals when the operation was over.

When the instrument of punishment was replaced in the depths of a drawer, Julia turned round and saw the lad on his knees close to her, shedding hot tears. It would have been foolish to ask him why he was weeping.

'You have repented of your error, haven't you,' she said, 'and you will be good from now on?'

'I don't want to any more . . . I don't want to any more . . .'

'You don't want to be wicked any more? You understand how disagreeable the results of an evil action are and you have decided to be good. Well, if you

213

keep to this resolution, I shan't give you any more of what you have just had.'

'I don't want to be beaten with a birch.'

'Oh, why do you prefer to be punished by hand?'

'Pauline always did it with her hand and afterwards . . .'

'Who is Pauline?'

'My big married sister.'

'And what did she do to you afterwards.'

'I don't know how to say it.'

'Try.'

'Do it with your hand, as you did the other day, and I'll show you.'

Julia bent over the boy and gave him a few light taps on the buttocks.

Pedro got hold of her hand and directed it towards the organ near the part affected by her corporal punishment. There with naive boldness he started to make her caress his prick which trembled and stiffened under her ministrations.

Madame de Corriero was quite amazed by what he was doing but also amused, so she let him go on.

'Do you find that pleasant?' she asked him.

'Oh, yes and if you do that to me afterwards, every time, I shall let you beat me whenever you like.'

Julia continued to lend herself to this entertainment, so much so, that the little devil became bolder and tried to slide his hand between the ribbons of Madame de Corriero's dressing-gown. He tore one of them in such a fortuitous way that one of her breasts was bared.

'Will you hold still, you naughty boy?' she said.

Pedro, his eyes shining like diamonds, set about sucking the lovely white breast facing him.

'Who taught you so well?' Madame de Corriero asked.

'Pauline did a bit; I saw her husband caress her but there are a lot of things I didn't understand. That's why I had a look to see how Claire's made, you remember that day on the grass bank.'

'And if we hadn't turned up what would have been the result of your examination?'

'I don't know, but I would have done what I used to do to Pauline when Manuel wasn't at home.'

'And what was that?'

'Hold on, I'll show you.'

Pedro slid to the floor.

'Don't move,' he said, 'you'll see how good it is, you'll cry out and go all pale, but let me do it.'

The little devil got on his knees, put his curly head under his guardian's light skirt and, there, very skilfully and very quickly, he made her utter cries of sheer ecstasy.

'Oh, the little devil,' she finally said, but not until she had achieved her paroxysm. Pedro then came out from his hiding place and Julia was not cruel enough to refuse him the kiss of thanks which his eyes demanded.

'Isn't it true that this makes women happy?' he said triumphantly.

'Quite possibly, you scamp, but if you should dare to say a word of any of this to anybody, it will be Pierre who will take care of your education in future.'

'Ah, you will see how obedient I shall be from now on. But you'll call me here from time to time, won't you?'

'To beat you, yes.'

'Oh, but not only for that.'

'We'll see, meanwhile put on your trousers and go for a walk.'

CHAPTER THIRTEEN

A month passed before Michel could join his beautiful lady at La Bidouze.

The result of this was that Julia spent more and more time with Claire, whom she no longer left alone with Pedro for a moment. As far as the latter was concerned, she no longer considered it appropriate to inflict manual punishment on him although he deserved it more than once. The memory of certain incidents connected with the last time she punished him made her reluctant to get Pierre to take her place.

The rascal might rebel and talk, she said to herself, and she waited for Michel to come and help her regularise the boy's position.

The well-beloved finally appeared and the days after his arrival were happy ones; decorum, as far as the servants were concerned, was preserved, but as Dorothy was privy to the secret it was easy to meet without arousing any suspicions. This was all the more so as the lodgings allocated to the young painter were in the same wing as that occupied by the mistress of the house.

So when evening came, the echoes in the long corridor of that isolated part of the house consisted of nothing but love talk. However, one evening an oath was heard. This was several days after Monsieur Lompret had arrived at La Bidouze.

After much love-making, he had fallen fast asleep by Julia's side, when suddenly a sharp pain in the shoulder woke him. He brought his hand to the painful spot and pulled out a toy dagger – at the same time he saw a shadow escaping by the light of the nightlamp.

'What is this?' he asked, jumping out of bed.

Julia lit some candles; they looked all around the room but found no one.

To have summoned the servants to carry out an investigation in the *château* would have compromised the mistress of the house. Michel said nothing. An idea fleetingly crossed his mind: was Julia deceiving him?

He repressed the thought as insulting to his mistress, but all the same he said to himself: 'Only a rival or a thief would play with a dagger like that; though it's true that the weapon used was nothing but a toy.'

He wondered who might have been responsible for the attack and, as he could find no plausible answer, he dismissed it from his mind. However, from that day on, he took care to bolt the doors when he was in Julia's room.

Madame de Corriero, for her part, guessed what it was all about. She had recognised the dagger which she had given to Pedro to complete his Spanish costume.

So the next day she profited from a moment of solitude to question him.

'What's happened to your dagger? You're not wearing it, have you lost it?'

'You know very well I haven't lost it, because you have got it.'

'So it was you, you wretch, who tried . . . ?'

'Yes.'

'And why did you do such a spiteful, wicked thing?'

'Because I spent some nights under your bed and I don't want you to embrace him the way you're doing.'

'Who are you talking about?'

'Monsieur Lompret, I hate him . . . you've never caressed me like that.'

'That's all we're short of. You know, Pedro, you should be careful, because if you start that again you will rue the day. Monsieur Lompret wishes you well; he will look after you and give you an education. You will become an artist like him, if you have the vocation, but you have to behave properly.'

Pedro did not reply but there were no tricks or acts of malice he did not expose Michel to. Julia had told him how she had found the scamp on the road. The artist's kind heart was moved; he fully entered into his friend's plans and they both agreed that Claire and Pedro should be taken to Paris.

However, one day Michel declared that he thought the time had come for the unruly Pedro, who tormented all the inhabitants of the house, to be punished severely. Next time, he decided, he would act as a good *paterfamilias* himself. He did not have long to wait. Michel was restoring a panel in Madame de Corriero's bedroom. His palette was ready, when he turned round and saw his persecutor mix the contents of one of his paint tubes with another. When he had finished that, he picked up another tube and was on the point of producing a most outrageous mixture of colours.

That morning, Michel could not conceal from himself that in all probability it was not Pierre who had placed a large lump of lard in each of his shoes; so, he put down the tools of his trade, went up to the lad, who had not seen him coming, put his hand on his shoulder and started to reprimand him. Drawn by the noise the raised voices were making, Julia appeared on the threshold of the room. Dorothy, too, arrived and said, 'Sir, I beg you, punish the imp who torments us from morning to night.'

Feeling sure of general approval, Michel decided he could not choose a better moment to assert his authority. He took the curtain cord which Dorothy obligingly offered him and used it to administer a chastisement which, this time, left traces on Pedro's fleshy parts for several days and was not followed by any kind of consolation.

Dorothy laughed with pleasure in her corner. So did Claire, though with less abandon because the critical situation of her play-mate reminded her of her own painful personal experience. As for Julia, she did not say anything to defend him.

Once the punishment had been inflicted, Michel took the youth by his belt and led him with his trousers half down to the corridor, where he came face to face with Pierre who mockingly asked him whether Monsieur had a lighter hand than Madame. Pale with rage and profoundly humiliated, the boy escaped to his room and that evening when they were looking for him they could not find him; he had disappeared.

'It's a good riddance,' Michel said to Julia when she told him. 'You would have had a lot of trouble with that brat, my friend.'

'As long as he's done nothing desperate.'

'What, just for a beating? Come now, he must have had much worse ones than the one he had this morning, I'll be bound. Let him take himself elsewhere.'

There was no more talk about Pedro at La Bidouze but his protectress, moved by a sentiment which it was difficult to analyse – pity, gratitude, curiosity about what time would do to the lad, all those things and others, as well, played their part – decided to ask the rural police to find him. It did not take them very long.

Without whispering a word of this to anyone, Julia spoke to him affectionately for a long time. What did she promise him? Perhaps the future will tell. However, for the present she took him to the Dominican Father Superior of Digne, told him what she knew about Pedro or, at least, some of it, because there were some details she did not go into, and asked him to turn the boy into an honest man.

'You will keep him confined to your establishment and let him pursue his studies at my expense. When he has graduated, one of your Fathers will bring him to me. From now on, Reverend Father, I ask you to supervise him extremely carefully because I think he is a most precocious youth.'

The Father Superior promised and the gates of the old college closed behind Pedro for a good many years to come.

CHAPTER FOURTEEN

Summer went by quickly under these conditions. Love lends wings to everything and there was astonishment at La Bidouze, when they found one day that the swallows had departed.

'Already.'

'Already, and now's the moment to follow their example; we too must leave,' Julia said.

'Where for?'

'Paris.'

They left for Paris where they enjoyed even more intimate and profound transports of love than they had ever known.

Michel loved Julia physically, that much is clear, but, above all, he loved her spiritually. Every day, he found more and more, that his thoughts merged more closely with hers in spite of the gaps there were in her knowledge.

Nature had endowed the young woman with a good mind, but there had been lacunae in her education. So he determined to initiate her into his own full, if austere, intellectual world. He persuaded her to leave Paris for the whole of the winter and made her visit Italy with its ancient and modern treasures and its hot sun, which seemed to deepen tenfold the stamp the country made on a man's soul – Italy, the true homeland of all those who want to think profound thoughts and love passionately! The lovers spent the following summer at La Bidouze and, the winter after that, Spain blessed them with the seductions of its climate and of its enchanting soil.

These prolonged absences had the fortunate effect of allowing Raoul de Paliseul's irritation to subside or at least to be deprived of a target. This was fortunate, because he continued to harbour resentment of Granada, so much so that he moved heaven and earth to find her, without anything ever occurring to give him the slightest clue to the mystery.

The affair between Maxence de Berny and Periwinkle had continued, though both were a little less enthusiastic about it now than when it had begun. All the same, they still met with pleasure in the rue Charles V. Too often, perhaps, because Florentine's health was suffering: she had become very pale and nervous. She worried her doctor, who advised her to remarry in the belief that sexual abstinence did not suit her temperament. Dorothy, who knew what was going on, shrugged her shoulders. Five years had thus passed without serious incident, five years of happiness. This is a term that destiny does not grant everyone and, if it does, it is rare for it to be renewed.

Madame de Corriero and Madame Vaudrez had drunk the cup of earthly happiness and left it a quarter full. The remainder would contain the dregs mixed with bitterness. It was Julia whom misfortune first befell.

One day, one of her friends introduced Monsieur de Paliseul to her; it came about in such a way that it could not be avoided without attracting attention.

'It doesn't matter, he won't recognise me,' she told herself.

And, in fact, he had never seen her features – but he *had* seen the faithful Dorothy without a mask. As he passed her in the hall, he recognised Madame Félicité Deschamps.

'Well, well,' he said in a mocking tone,' we seem to have come down in the world, mistress mine. This is a fine house but all the same, when you have had your own place, it must be hard to live below stairs in another's.'

Dorothy pretended not to understand and said the viscount must be joking. Pierre, who was present at the scene did not miss a word of the dialogue, supported her in swearing that Dorothy, like him, had been in Madame de Corriero's service for ten years. Paliseul was too certain that he had not been mistaken not to listen attentively.

'For ten years!'

These words seemed to shed a ray of light on the matter. Perhaps it was her mistress who was the beautiful Granada.

He carefully observed Madame de Corriero and took note of every slightest detail. He became convinced that Julia, whose virtue everybody praised, was the voluptuous woman whom he had possessed one night in the rue Charles V. He had her spied on, paid a man to follow her and in less than a month he knew all about her love affair with Michel and their trysting place in the rue Charles V. He wanted to take his revenge on her and pretended to be a fervent admirer of the young woman's. He spoke about her at every opportunity with a kind of discreet silliness, smiling perfidiously and spreading a thousand spiteful insinuations about her which were so subtle nobody could put a finger on them.

Julia, without knowing why, soon noticed a number of her acquaintances were dropping her: people cooled towards her, the women appeared hostile and the men over-friendly. The atmosphere of sympathy and of respect in which she had lived until then, changed. Michel, who regularly called at several houses belonging to his circle of friends, noticed the same thing and both of them wondered what these rather frightening symptoms might mean.

'Could our connection have become common knowledge?' Julia asked.

'That wouldn't be enough to account for it. Ninety per cent of the women you receive are in the same position, give or take a few variations. It isn't that; it must be something else.'

One evening this something else was revealed. One of Julia's friends gave a big party. Gradually the guests who were not dancing dispersed, some to the library, others to the orangery. Soon, among the latter, a group was formed made up of Maxence de Berny, Melreuse, Paliseul and two or three other Artichokes who started to gossip like old women about all the Society ladies there.

Michel, who was sitting apart hidden by some shrubs, did not miss a word of their conversation.

'Come, Paliseul,' Melreuse said, 'calm down and don't give rein to your malicious strain. In any case, we can't take seriously what you tell us about the lady. We have known you too long, my friend, and your story is the counterpart of the one you told us about the beautiful Granada, that ravishing houri from the rue Charles V who turned out to be not a beautiful lady at all and whose twentieth birthday had taken place so long before that it was lost in the mists of time.'

The mention of the rue Charles V made Michel prick up his ears and go pale.

'Ah, gentlemen, do stop laughing,' Paliseul said. 'Appearances are deceptive and sometimes a gallant gentleman prefers to allow himself to be accused rather than compromise a lady.'

'So the mysterious Granada is not a myth?' one of the gentlemen asked.

'If he insists on it,' Maxence said, 'let us leave him his illusions.' He was beginning to find that they were getting on to dangerous ground and wanted to change the subject.'

'If I insist on it, it is because I have my reasons for it.'

'You remember, gentlemen,' Melreuse said, 'the superb buttocks which that lady showed us and, my God, how daringly she proved to us that she was not black.'

Paliseul was still sniggering.

'Laugh your heads off but remember: he who laughs last laughs longest.'

Suddenly the outline of Madame de Corriero could be seen in the half-open door.

'Charming lady,' one of the gentlemen said, 'it's a pity you get your wings burnt if you approach too close to her.'

Paliseul was still sniggering.

'Oh,' Melreuse said, 'there must be a lover somewhere. I have heard about a painter who frequently calls on her and on her sister, Madame Vaudrez.'

Paliseul was still sniggering.

'Oh, do stop it,' Maxence said impatiently, 'you are irritating us with your nervous laugh. I expect you've got something unpleasant to say. Just forget about it and let's get on to another subject.

'Have you noticed,' Paliseul asked, ignoring Maxence's remarks, 'the remarkable resemblance between Madame de Corriero's faithful lady's maid and Madame Félicité Deschamps of the rue Charles V?'

'Dorothy?' Maxence exclaimed. 'You are dreaming.'

'What, the lady who held you so tenderly in her arms on that beautiful plush-covered bed decorated with pomegranate leaves?'

'Yes.'

'Yes, it's true,' somebody said.

'Nonsense,' said another, 'how could that beautiful room belong to her?'

A whole field of conjecture opened up for the Artichokes and Madame de Corriero's name was on everyone's lips.

'Well, gentlemen, is it not possible,' Paliseul said, 'that I was not as unfortunate as you seem to think? For ten years the faithful Dorothy has been Madame de Corriero's lady's maid.'

'What you are doing, Raoul, is unworthy of you,' Maxence said. 'To satisfy your pride, you disinter an old adventure in a way that might do harm to a woman. Luckily, we are not the kind of people who take that kind of joke seriously.'

'Take it as you like, gentlemen, but keep your pity for those who are more unfortunate than myself even in respect of my love affair with the beautiful Granada. She is a delicious woman and I consider the handsome Michel Lompret, my successor, to be a very fortunate creature.'

'Excuse me, gentlemen,' Michel suddenly said, rising like a spring from the couch on which he was sitting, 'excuse me, but you have just mentioned my name and in a tone I dislike; would you please refrain from mentioning it in future.'

'Oh, you were there all the time.'

'But, my dear sir,' Maxence said in a conciliatory tone, 'we said nothing disagreeable about you.'

226

'Agreeable or disagreeable, I repeat to Monsieur de Paliseul my injunction not to use my name again.'

This was said in a very sharp tone.

'I am not in the habit of taking lessons from anyone,' Paliseul said.

'There is a first time for everything and if you don't like the lesson I'm giving you perhaps you would prefer this one.'

With these words, Michel made a gesture with his glove of slapping the viscount's face.

'That will do, sir, my seconds will call on yours tomorrow.'

Greetings were exchanged and they parted.

'What folly,' Maxence said very angrily, 'to tell stories about women without looking behind the shrubs, as if such conversations were not dynamite.'

'And all this because of a misunderstanding,' Lyncent said.

'No, gentlemen, not because of a misunderstanding. Madame de Corriero is the Granada of the rue Charles V and her lover, Monsieur de Lompret, did not know that I had been selected before him. The discovery hurt him and that is why tomorrow I shall run him through.'

In fact, Michel was stricken to the heart when he learned that Julia, this woman who had been his and with whom he had lived in perfect communion for five years, could conceal something from him. It was exceedingly painful for him to discover that the conceited Paliseul had experienced the same intoxication as he had himself and that he had the right, when he saw Madame de Corriero, to remember a thousand intimate details and to tell his friends about them if he were indelicate enough to do so. He went back to his house deeply hurt; he saw the beautiful illusions of his love disappear through the wound in his heart.

He had the courage to hide his feelings and went at the usual hour not to the rue Charles V, but to the boulevard St-Michel. There, without telling Julia that he would be duelling the following day, he spoke to her of everyday matters. Still she was struck by his pallor and also by the sad kiss he gave her when he left, which was like a farewell.

'What is the matter with you?' she asked.

Michel was on the point of asking her, 'Have you really given yourself to Monsieur de Paliseul, if only for one night?' but he did not want to make her blush and he left without saying it. But a doubt remained in his mind. 'After all,' he thought, 'what if that conceited fellow had lied. He did not produce any positive proofs, so let's find out what we can from Dorothy.'

Making a superhuman effort to overcome his emotion, he asked her to come and speak to him in his studio because he had a surprise that he was preparing for Madame. Dorothy obeyed and there, laughingly as if it were of no importance, he joked about the beautiful bottom she had shown the gentlemen.

'Tell me, Dorothy,' he said to the lady's maid when he saw she had no suspicion, 'why on earth did Madame treat this poor infatuated viscount so badly? After all he's quite a good-looking fellow, well-mannered, too, and I have never been able to understand why he fell into such disfavour.'

'Are you complaining about it?'

'God forbid, but I have always wondered why.'

'Oh,' said Dorothy with a laugh, 'he just wasn't her type, that's what it often comes down to in matters of love.'

'Perhaps you are right,' Michel replied, as if it were a matter of no moment. He gave her the little box he had previously prepared for Julia and sent her away. He no longer had any doubt that his idol had feet of clay. Who could tell whether he who loved her so much, with all his heart, had not been loved in return only because he happened to be 'her type', as Dorothy so brutally put it. This idea tortured him.

'Come now,' he told himself. 'I have lived long enough; I should have died yesterday.'

The following day the same studio that had witnessed the first manifestations of the only love of his life, the scene of so many delightful dreams and exquisite realities, seemed to be mournful because it was reduced to sheltering Michel's body. He was brought back home, pierced by a sword-thrust which Raoul de Paliseul had inflicted without causing much pain. He had still been alive when his friend laid him on the bed on which Julia and he liked to stretch out. Pegleg, half-crazed with grief, wanted to let the world know what had happened, but he did not know Madame de Corriero's address.

When she heard about the duel from Florentine, and rushed to Michel's place, worried to death. When she arrived, he had just breathed his last without leaving a word for her and without a sigh of regret for the existence he was leaving behind – when in full possession of his youth and his talent.

CHAPTER FIFTEEN

This premature death was a terrible blow to Julia de Corriero. She had loved Michel sincerely and the end of their relationship, which had been so intimate and so sweet, could not fail to break her heart in a dreadful way. Every part of her was affected, the very fibres of her mind suffered, because there was not a single thought of hers with which she did not associate her friend.

The reasons for the duel had been concealed from her, but a malicious hand took care, by means of an anonymous letter, to let her know that she alone was the reason for Monsieur Lompret's intervening in the Artichokes' conversation; she was also informed that Michel took hardly any steps to defend himself.

'He will have died cursing me' she told herself.

There was no help for it: the poor broken spirit felt the need that all those who suffer have, that of self-inflicted pain.

For six months those around Madame de Corriero did not know whether her weakened state of health would be able to resist the shock she had undergone.

She hardly paid attention to what was going on around her and did not notice the gaps that appeared in her drawing-room. Surrounded as she was by the tender care of Florentine and defended against all by the respectful sympathy of Maxence de Berny, Julia recovered a little when the fine days began. Her friends took advantage of this and took her to *Les Charmettes* where her love of life gained the upper hand. The future no longer looked completely bleak. Her pain and her sickness had altered her beauty and a profound sadness enveloped her heart. Julia exercised self-control and bid farewell to the great joys of this world. She transferred to Claire, whom she had not stopped looking after, all the overflowing affection of her heart.

'In a year's time, I shall take her out of boarding school,' she said to herself, 'she is a good and gentle girl and she loves me. Her presence will banish my loneliness.'

The young girl spent all her holidays with her protectress and her youth and gaiety lit the house up like a sunray – a pale autumnal sun, if you like, but still one with enough heat to warm Madame de Corriero's poor, tortured heart.

Two years passed and time had done its work to heal the wounds of Michel's death. Julia still cried often, in secret, but as far as the outside world was concerned, her lips had again found the pretty smile of her happy days. That year she moved to La Bidouze with a relatively light heart.

She loved that house set in the middle of woods and rocks and she never failed to take up her summer quarters there as soon as May brought out the lilac blossom. It was there, in the sub-tropical heat, that one afternoon she saw in the drive a monk in the white cassock of a Dominican, accompanied by the fine figure of a tall, bearded young man.

The Reverend Father Martin and his pupil, Monsieur Pedro, were soon announced. Madame de Corriero had never abandoned her ward but she did not want to see him again before he had finished both his leaving examinations. The day before he had brilliantly gained his diploma in science, having taken his diploma in the arts the year before, and now the Father Superior of the college had sent him to his benefactress, his godmother, as he had decided to call Julia.

The boy had profited from the tuition he had been given. To begin with, it had been difficult to tame his gipsy temperament, which was totally undisciplined and precocious, but Julia's promise to him constantly stimulated his will and when the severity of his masters seemed unbearable and the work too tedious, he thought of the mistress of La Bidouze and told himself, 'When I am grown up and if I achieve something . . . she promised me . . . she will be the first . . .' and Pedro gave all that the school asked of him.

Julia dimly recalled the bait by means of which the transformation of the young scamp into a fine young man had been achieved. She received the new graduate very cordially, thanked the Reverend Father for his pains and announced her intention of keeping Pedro with her at La Bidouze until the start of term at the Polytechnic, an establishment where she proposed that he should continue his studies and train for a career. The Reverend Father left, generously rewarded, and Pedro took possession of a set of rooms intended for him: a pretty bedroom and a sitting-room, which Madame de Corriero had turned into a study for him. That very night she ordered from Paris everything needed to complete a young person's first great joy, that of freedom: good books in a library to which he had the key, his own things in his own rooms, an excellent sporting gun, a good dog and a fine horse.

It had been Madame de Corriero's intention to

divide her fortune between Claire and Pedro and to marry them off if they loved each other, so that evening she was not a little perplexed when she saw Pedro suddenly kneel before her and kiss her hands. All afternoon, during dinner and their walk in the park, she had talked to him and realised that he had developed very fine qualities of heart and mind. The school had weeded the garden of his personality and now only the finest plants were left. Pedro had the makings of a man in the fullest sense of the word.

'Well,' she said to herself, 'it was a good thing I did that day when, after beating him, I gave him my promise . . . decidedly, whether they are big or small, that is the way to influence them . . . I did promise . . . and he does not appear to have forgotten.'

Julia reflected for a while and, becoming very serious, she told herself. 'Well, I'll keep my promise and I'll teach him what my poor Michel had understood so well, that voluptuousness attains its culmination only when its actions are directed both by the imagination and the heart. The electric shock produced by the contact of two sets of skin is not enough – a divine spark is needed. Let us complete our work with this child who owes to me his first amorous sensations as he owes everything else to me. I shall arm him against the pitfalls of life, lest he stray in the paths of vulgar sensuality, and teach him voluptuousness without cynicism and obscenity.

The amorous skill of a man, his delicacy of expression and that which makes the women he loves, if only on one single occasion, remember him for the rest of their lives – all those things depend on the first woman he possesses. But what am I thinking about? In spite of his attitude this afternoon, he probably remembers nothing. If so, I shall watch over his choice because I want my little Claire to be happy with a good husband.'

Julia had these thoughts, while Dorothy was helping her undress in the same dressing-room at La Bidouze where Pedro a long time ago experienced his godmother's severity.

Dorothy withdrew, when her work was done, and Madame de Corriero – in a long muslin dressing-gown – rested her elbows on the sill of the open window. She raised her eyes to look at that lovely southern night twinkling with stars, let her gaze rest on the dark mass of trees, and luxuriantly inhaled the fresh breezes, scented with the odours of the garden, which blew over her face.

She heard a slight sound from the corridor and almost immediately caressing and trembling arms were round her waist. Madame de Corriero half turned and saw without much surprise that it was Pedro.

'Godmother,' he said with an emotion so great, he could scarcely suppress it – 'I love you.'

'I love you, too, my dear boy, but we have time to tell each other that, and this is not an appropriate hour to come to me.'

'I love you, Godmother,' the young man repeated, 'and when will the hour be more appropriate to tell you that? Look at the calm which surrounds us, listen to the murmur from the sleeping earth all around. We are alone, quite alone. I was a poor gipsy boy the day you took me in, starving to death down there on that path, which we can see from here in the moonlight. I would have become a criminal if you had been disgusted by my viciousness and had abandoned me. Instead you took care of me. You have made of me what I am. All my being belongs to you . . . but I should have preferred not to have the benefit of your

234

benevolence if tonight you extinguish in my heart this flame of hope which is the sacred flame to which I consecrated all the efforts of my college life. It alone brought about the efforts which I made . . . that hope . . . you know what hope, Godmother.'

Julia knew, but she wanted to be told.

During the day she had banished all formality between herself and Pedro and, like a mother, insisted that he use the familiar '*tu*' when speaking to her. 'Explain yourself, dear Pedro.'

'Oh have you forgotten? You made me a promise . . . when the rural police had found me, you took me to the little pavilion at the end of the park. There, after speaking to me as if you loved me, you punished me severely but in my mind I felt that I deserved it and I didn't mind. Afterwards we were alone. I had been punished but not humiliated. After my chastisement, even before I had got dressed, you took me on your knees and told me things I could never forget. I understood that if you did not spare me punishment this was not from malice but because you loved me and when you put your hands on my burning flesh I experienced a sensation so delicious that, while still weeping, I turned round in your arms without taking any notice of my nudity.

'It was at that moment, Godmother, that you promised me if I behaved well . . . I can still feel your hands caress me but not, that time, to soothe the pain of a beating but to reveal to me the mysteries of love. It is this promise that I ask you to keep now.'

'Have you really never . . . ?'

'No, it would be impossible for a woman to enter the monastery.'

'What about anybody else . . . ?'

'Not that, either. It was difficult to resist that temptation. However, as you had told me that I would be

235

nothing but a poor and miserable creature if I could not master my flesh, I fought against it. But today I don't want to fight any more . . . make yourself my good fairy godmother to the very end. Teach me not to love — that would be pointless because I already know that — but teach me to express what I feel so strongly.'

Julia had always regretted that in her life there had not been an episode similar to that in Florentine's. Cherubino's virginity had more than once been the subject of her dreams. Pedro's speech was too close to her secret longings for her to hesitate too long.

She took him in her arms and in turn, looked into his eyes.

The youth had become a man, a chaste man whose impetuous blood was seething; the crisis could not be delayed too long: it was developing at a headlong rate. Nor did Madame de Corriero try to do so. With one hand she motioned Pedro to undress and involuntarily she remembered the scene in which she gave him a similar order in the same dressing-room, but with a completely different aim. This time he did not wait to be asked again as on the day when it was a matter of making the acquaintance of the terrible birch which he disliked so much. His jacket and trousers were quickly discarded, uncovering his slender but robust and well-proportioned body. Julia slid her bare arm from under her shift and drew him to her. Nervous shivers ran over Pedro's skin, his nostrils dilated, and sighs resembling moans, came from his chest. Julia quickly got rid of his vest, which joined his coat and trousers, and the young man showed himself to her in all his splendid young nudity.

'You are good-looking,' she said as she lifted herself up and pressed him against her chest.

Julia's dressing-gown was one of those intelligent

garments which only tied ribbons kept in place. The fine muslin, which veiled her body – still beautiful in spite of the combined action of sorrow and of time – scarcely kept in position, and Pedro quickly bared her white breasts which he smothered in passionate kisses.

'Come here, right up against me, my darling,' Julia, who was beginning to reciprocate his passion, said, 'with your chest against mine, your lips on mine, your breath mingling with mine, your tongue searching mine . . . put your hand here under my back, raising it when you want – and there, there, inside me, come and receive from the depth of my being the baptism of my fluid of love, come and drown me with yours and savour the delight of your first kiss of love.'

Pedro was a little clumsy, but his protectress was forgiving and directed his organ of love towards the grotto where his initiation needed to be completed. The happy Pedro soon found himself surrounded by hot pressure which gave him a new and delicious sensation. All his nerves tensed from the nape of his neck to the soles of his feet and he was shaken as if by the shock of an electric battery.

Julia had let herself slide a little on the wide and solid piece of furniture which served as the stage of their love-making; her legs apart, she responded to Pedro's movements in the depth of her entrails, while with his finger placed on her clitoris she directed his vibrations in order to be able to join simultaneously in the moan of love with which her ears were going to be assailed.

It did not take long. Pedro was very soon overwhelmed by that feeling which was close to pain, so intense is it, and from his panting chest came the first roar of sexual frenzy he had ever shouted out. He wanted to stay intertwined with Julia for a long time: he found the feel of the scented flesh of a woman close

237

to his, delicious. The first crisis of love usually leaves a man with a great nervous fatigue, succeeded by a delightful state of languor. This is rarely appreciated by a woman; so, very quickly, Madame de Corriero dismissed her young lover, reserving to herself the right to give him more advanced lessons at her leisure. He had just loved and experienced joy but he still had to learn to make his partner experience it as well.

During the three months he spent at La Bidouze she inculcated into him sound principles: theory was generally followed by practical experiments and she taught him never to hurry developments and never to delay them for too long.

With few exceptions, men do not make love well. Often they complain of the frigidity of women and in this they are like an ignoramus who complains that his violin does not produce any melody, when the only trouble is that he does not know how to play it. The way in which one undresses a woman is by itself enough to make her freeze or to set her alight. Letting her take off her own garments is a mistake and taking them off quickly and too briskly is another. That delicate operation must be savoured like the kisses that accompany it.

Going too fast to the desired end is an act of selfishness. What is necessary is to make sure beforehand that there is magnetic tension in the lips, the breath and the breasts. It is essential, with a knowing kiss, to excite the little hillock of love, which is the coping stone of voluptuous sensation but which in some women, though they are very impressionable, is not developed sufficiently for the approach of the man to bring about the final spasm. As long as the lips and the tongue have done their work in advance, then it is possible to carry on in lively fashion and the well-informed will not find as many frigid women as the ill-informed believe exist.

Julia did not deprave Pedro: she left him in ignorance of the obscene practices of libertinage, but she taught him all the refinements of voluptuousness with the care of a mother, teacher and lover combined. She allowed the noble and natural chords of this child to vibrate and when he left her to start work in the Polytechnic she was convinced with good reason that he was both armed against venal love and trained to become that rare specimen who, having the name of lover, is really worthy of that name.

The day before the beginning of term Mādame de Corriero had a long talk with Pedro. She spoke to him about his future and told him that the field of love was for the time being closed to him, that he would have to work hard and that he would not see her until he started on the career that had been planned for him. The young man protested but he had known for a long time that his godmother's charm concealed a will of iron. Once she had made up her mind, there was nothing for it but to obey.

Two years passed. He had just graduated from the polytechnic as a civil engineer. A word from Madame de Corriero recalled him to La Bidouze. The evening of his arrival, when he knocked at the door of her rooms, he found it shut and bolted and the next day Julia told him that what had been very pleasant some time earlier was now almost hateful to her.

'Youth calls to youth, my friend. Always remember your old godmother with affection, your godmother who beat you when you were a naughty boy and who later taught you to become a man, but from now on save your love for one whose heart can respond to the vigour of your own.

'The future, happiness, love — they are all there,'

239

Julia ended her speech, pointing to Claire who was coming towards them. Pedro tried only feebly to make his godmother reconsider her decision. The young girl's vernal radiance was such, that it quite put into the shade Madame de Corriero's autumnal charms.

What she had hoped for happened. The two children fell in love with each other and the sight of their tenderness, that little fresh and pure romance being written under her very eyes into the great volume of destiny, pleased her greatly.

Before leaving La Bidouze, she saw Pedro married to Claire after she had given them a property which was part of her estate. The marble quarry that formed part of it was enough to occupy the young engineer and to support the material needs of the household.

'I believe I have made two people happy,' Madame de Corriero said to herself, when she had left her protégés – who had come to see her off at the station, on her departure for Paris.

CHAPTER SIXTEEN

From time to time Julia still liked to go to the house in the rue Charles V and to sit alone in the room which had seen so much happiness. There she recalled memories of the past and wept occasionally. More often she delighted in these day-dreams which were no longer full of the bitter and deep despair of the first moments of pain, although her wounds had not healed completely.

This particular day she had been reading a great deal, which did not have the effect of calming her mind or her senses. In this temple of voluptuousness, erected by her own efforts and Florentine's in the Marais, there was a library – not exactly suitable for a girls' boarding school. By chance it contained the travel memoirs of a writer who had anticipated and, indeed, gone beyond, our epoch of extreme naturalism and described the habits and customs of Africa with a wealth of detail that might have made Zola go pale with envy. Idleness had put this volume into the hands of Madame de Corriero who after a few moments of reading found herself engrossed. The book added a new spice to her imagination. The author, who was favourably disposed towards the natives, stated that carnal contact between the two races, the white and the black, resulted in veritable treasures of voluptuousness. According to this eccentric, the

241

penetrating effluvia of the black race produce love juices infinitely superior to those of any other, in their ability to excite amorous sensations. He let his pen run on under the influence of his memories and produced a mass of details to support his argument. When she had finished the book, Madame de Corriero became thoughtful.

'That's odd,' she said to herself, 'I had always thought that a white woman would feel repelled by such an approach.'

The day had come to an end and the weather was stormy. The young woman was lying on a *chaise longue*, dressed in nothing but a chiffon dressing-gown and gazing vacantly into space, when suddenly the door opened and Patrick, the coachman who drove the sphinx-emblazoned carriage, came in carrying a torch. Patrick was twenty-five years old – a superbly made black man, more handsome than his fellows. He did not speak but he was not deaf. He put the candelabra on the table which was next to Julia and went towards the window to shut it, pointing at the same time to the black clouds which were massing on the horizon. Julia made a gesture of approval and looked at Patrick with more attention than she had ever done until then. What she had just read was exercising her mind.

'The fact is,' she said to herself, 'that there are fine-looking black men. The question of colour apart, this one is astonishing.'

Patrick – tall, slender with an intelligent look – seemed to her quite different from his fellow blacks. A strange and astonishing thought occurred to Madame de Corriero, who was tired of suffering and of having her senses dulled for so long.

'In the last resort, it really doesn't matter with a man like that,' she told herself.

Patrick had been brought up by the General, who had found him goodness knows where, and had given him some sort of education.

'Patrick,' she suddenly called out.

The negro, who was on the point of leaving the room, turned back.

'Sit down there,' she said and pointed to the bear-skin on which her feet were resting.

The black man stared at his mistress in astonishment and obeyed. Julia amused herself by passing her hand over his crinkly hair, which moved Patrick a great deal. He paled under his black skin and his eyes became bloodshot. Julia moved her slender fingers in his fleece of hair and breathed in its scent, which she was astonished to find was not disagreeable. She then lent over the young man's head and placed a kiss on his forehead. Patrick was absolutely taken aback and started to tremble.

'Go and shut the door,' Julia ordered.

Patrick obeyed and, more and more dumbfounded, remained standing up in a corner.

'Come here and sit down close to me.'

Patrick approached. Julia stretched out her foot and motioned him to take off her shoes. When the shoes had been removed, she pointed to her stockings, which her new kind of lady's maid also removed, being very careful not to touch his young mistress's bare legs. After the stockings, it was the turn of the dress and the waist petticoats. Quite soon she was not wearing anything but her slip. Julia now gestured to Patrick to remove his coat, then his waistcoat and then . . . his trousers – which was not done without a certain amount of resistance on his part.

'I wish it,' Julia said.

The servant, accustomed to passive submission, was almost in tears as he did what he was told, telling himself that sorrow had probably deranged Madame's mind. Patrick's shoes followed his trousers.

When he had nothing left on his body but his vest, Julia with a nervous gesture undressed completely and made him take off his last garment. She found herself face to face with a magnificent ebony figure. He contemplated her with a look in which respect was beginning to retreat before sexual desire. His hands remained idle but his instrument of love stood up long, strong, well-made and full of promise. Julia, having looked at it for a moment, put her lips on Patrick's who felt the last of his respect leave him as he understood what sweet service was expected of him.

'Love me as if I were one of your countrywomen,' Julia said.

Patrick lowered his head and fell to his knees as a sign of submission, then he kissed the legs and the feet of the young woman while shaking his body as a sign of contentment. After that he took her in his arms like a child, rocked her, covered her breasts with kisses and . . . Julia felt a desire for a strange and bizarre sexual experience rising in her.

Patrick was mute; had he not been, he would certainly have murmured some weird endearment. Soon a hot fire succeeded the tremors that passed over Madame de Corriero's skin. Patrick would have made a whole monastery of monks envious with his fine erection. With an indescribable gesture Julia seized the erect member and drew her partner to the bed. Patrick understood that the moment of action had arrived. With a nervous arm, he laid his mistress on the mattress, gave her a prolonged kiss on the clitoris of the charming cunt that presented itself to his view and savoured the joy of possessing a beautiful white woman — something which had never happened to him before.

The travel writer had not lied altogether.

Julia experienced a very special sexual spasm which was followed by lively surprise when she saw that her servant, as soon as he had recovered from his orgasm, threw himself upon the scene of his exploits again, and with an agile and careful tongue, removed every trace of his previous presence there. No cat cleans its kittens more carefully just after they are born. This exercise in cleanliness had the foreseeable result. Julia's senses, deprived for so long, awoke with a ferocious appetite and Patrick was obliged to get to work again to appease them. This happened a good many times because Patrick, in his house-proud way, cleared up each time with his busy tongue, which excited his partner anew.

But everything down on this earth must come to an end. Julia was sated and dismissed her servant. It was high time, too. The brilliant engine of war which only an hour beforehand had stood up triumphantly, was now piteous to behold.

Despite his fatigue, Patrick did not shut his eyes before one o'clock in the morning. As for Julia, she told herself that the traveller had not exaggerated the prowess of black men. All the same, contrary to Patrick's hopes, this turned out to have been a unique evening, never followed by another.

CHAPTER SEVENTEEN

Julia had experienced the shocks of life. Florentine, for her part, was beginning to feel the first stirrings of the north wind. Her affair with Maxence was still going on, but every week her health seemed to be more undermined. She was getting close to thirty and the crisis of her sexual energy was upon her. Her doctor thought it necessary to take Madame de Corriero into his confidence regarding his worries about her sister. According to him, it was urgent for the young woman to get married.

'She must become a mother again,' he said 'or I shan't be responsible for the consequences. The gravest nervous disorders might well arise.'

'And you think motherhood will . . . ?'

'Its preliminaries at least would be useful,' the doctor said with a smile.

Dorothy had for long been forecasting that no good would come from the existing state of affairs, so it was agreed that an attempt would be made to persuade Florentine to break with Maxence. Nothing kept Madame Vaudrez with him except force of habit. The good fellow was quite often unfaithful to her, a fact of which she was not unaware. All the same, she could not be persuaded.

So Julia took matters into her own hands and practically kidnapped Madame Vaudrez to take her to La

Bidouze. At the same time she informed Maxence of the situation and asked him not to press Florentine to stay with him.

The entire little colony went on its way and soon Florentine's cheeks took on some colour. This made Julia happy and the summer passed without any remarkable incidents, one might even say somewhat monotonously. So one day the ladies decided to spend a few weeks at Saint-Jean-de-Luz before taking up their winter quarters.

There were an enormous number of people in the spa that year. Frenchmen, foreigners, everybody seemed to have decided to meet there. The ladies were taking a walk in the outskirts of the town when suddenly at a crossroads two cries were heard:

'Madame Vaudrez!'

'Cherub . . . the Duke of Hérissey!'

Gaétan, for it was he, smiled and at the same time gave Madame Vaudrez a look which was both curious and full of tender memories.

'Well met, have you been here for some time?'

'Yes, let me introduce my son.'

'Our Cherubino,' Julia said maliciously.

'He is well-named, Madame, because he looks like a little angel.'

And Gaétan planted two affectionate kisses on the cheeks of the child who looked at him with surprise.

'And where have you come from?'

'From Japan. You haven't forgotten that my mother wanted me to tour the world ten years ago to shelter me from the temptations of Paris. I am now tired of travelling and am returning to Paris and propose to live there like a respectable property owner.'

'I hope we will meet often,' the two sisters said to him.

'Every day if you don't chase me away. But, meanwhile perhaps you will allow me to spoil Cherubino a little,' he said, addressing Florentine.

'Willingly, but not too much: he is already as stubborn as a mule.'

'He takes after his Papa,' Gaétan said with a laugh.

'And that?' Julia asked caressing the child's blonde locks.

'He gets those from his mother,' Florentine said in the same tone.

'Ladies,' the Duke of Hérissey said after talking to them for a little while longer, 'please excuse me. I have an appointment with a friend of mine at three o'clock. Tonight, I shall present him to you if you will allow me.'

'Strange meeting,' Julia said when the young man had gone.

'Indeed,' Florentine replied thoughtfully.

'Whom is he going to introduce to us?'

'Some islander picked up on his journeys, I expect.'

But it turned out to be no islander. To the utter astonishment of the two sisters it was none other than — Viscount Saski. It was certainly the viscount but the years had taken a heavy toll of him. The old, handsome Gaston no longer existed. He was still the same well-mannered Polish nobleman but now he was bald, his fine beard was sprinkled with threads of silver, his face was lined and the shadows round his eyes testified to the great sorrows that had beset him. For him, too, the season of laughter and of love had ended. He had lost his wife after an unhappy marriage that lasted some years. His children had died and his life had been full of tribulations of all kinds.

Only Aunt Wilhelmine Saska had survived among those close to him. She had got a great deal weaker because she could no longer digest her daily chicken without difficulty and, as she was stubborn about keeping to her accustomed diet, she had contracted severe gastritis.

Julia and he looked at each other for a long time with different feelings to begin with, but later they merged into one common thought: he has suffered . . . she has wept . . . and . . . their hands grasped each other.

'Have you forgiven me?' he asked. 'Fate has punished me.'

'I have forgotten,' Julia replied simply.

Six months later in the courtyard of *Les Charmettes*, carriages filled with luggage were drawn up. Not far away, two men gave orders to the servants. One of them was the Duke of Hérissey, since that morning Madame Vaudrez' husband, the other Viscount Saski, now married to Madame de Corriero. Near the drawing-room window the two brides stood in its embrasure, shaking hands and evidently bidding each other farewell. They were no longer the young women we met at the beginning of this account; both had attained maturity and their outward appearance, too, had changed.

April was no longer, as then, singing its joyful song of spring. Autumn was approaching its end and the first winter winds were blowing the leaves off the trees and on to the ground in sad swells.

'Do you remember, Julia,' Florentine said, 'our lovely fledgling flights towards happiness?'

'Yes,' Julia replied sadly, 'but I want to forget them.'

'We are starting a new stage of life, my darling.'

'Indeed, after a summer storm of blossoms, we shall now have to face the blizzards of winter and, after that, we shall come to that unknown port towards which we are sailing.'

The two women tearfully embraced.

'Come now, be of good courage,' Julia said, 'let us say farewell to the past, farewell to our youth, farewell to the intoxications of happiness and of love. Our suns are setting; the rays of dawn are no longer for us.'

'It is sad,' Florentine said, embracing her sister again, 'our hearts are desolate, even dead, but all the same there will be people who, when they see us in the arms of our husbands, will conclude that proverbs really do tell the truth — *on revient toujours à ses premiers amours* — people always return to their first love.